Death
by
Podcasting

Sarah Archer & Landis Wade

Death by Podcasting

ISBN eBook: 979-8-9877570-6-2
ISBN paperback: 979-8-9877570-7-9
Library of Congress Control Number: 2023917833

Cover design: Dissect Designs
Book design: Jennipher Tripp
Publisher: Charlotte Readers Podcast, LLC

Learn more about author Sarah Archer at: saraharcherwrites.com
Learn more about author Landis Wade at: landiswade.com
Learn more about the podcast at: charlottereaderspodcast.com

Printed in the United States of America

To podcasters everywhere.
Be careful out there.

PRAISE FOR *THE PLUS ONE*

Readers who think they don't like romance and those who think they don't like science fiction may be astonished to discover themselves loving the combination in Sarah Archer's irresistible, unputdownable, comic, debut romance novel.

— **Booklist** (starred review)

In her debut novel, Archer concocts an endearingly unlucky-at-love heroine…A fun story that will appeal to geeks and beach-goers alike.

— **Kirkus Reviews**

PRAISE FOR *DEADLY DECLARATIONS*

Deadly Declarations is what you'd get if *National Treasure* and *The Firm* had a book baby. Part historical mystery, part courtroom drama, part Scooby gang romp, 100 percent whip-smart, engaging, and deliciously unputdownable. Two thumbs up!

—**Tracy Clark**, multi-nominated Anthony, Shamus, and Lefty Award finalist and winner of the 2020 Sue Grafton Memorial Award for the Cass Raines Chicago Mystery Series

Landis Wade has given us a page turner, a novel rooted in history and mystery and imagination. This is a crackling good book.

— **Frye Gaillard**, American historian and author of *A Hard Rain: America in the 1960s*

Most podcasts live a short life. They're created in a fit of passion, but once the excitement fades, so does the devotion. It's a lonely death.

— **Brian Baltosiewich**, Queen City Podcast Network founder and producer

TAKE 1

KILLER FEEDBACK

In six years of podcasting, Raspy Fuse had received many text messages, but never a death threat. He'd been editing the morning's audio recordings when the text arrived. He'd read it twice already, and now he read it a third time.

> Good afternoon, Raspy. As a long-time literary podcast listener who knows the written word, I can honestly say the Under the Covers show is one of the best. Your guests are top-notch, the genre variety keeps things fresh, and the chemistry between you and Salty Remarks—is that really her given name? —is unmatched. Not to be dramatic— more like deadly accurate—I am writing to warn you that one of the three author guests you and Salty plan to interview Tuesday night intends to kill you both. Congratulations on your recent detective novel. It's your best yet.

Raspy took off his headphones and leaned back in his worn leather chair. He looked around his apartment, where posters of his favorite books graced the walls: John le Carré's *The Spy Who Came in from the Cold*, Tana French's *In the Woods*, and Agatha Christie's *And Then There Were None*. The text was more suited to a mystery novel than real life. He said the words "kill you both" out loud, which he realized as soon as he'd done it was a mistake. He first heard the squawk and flap of feathers by his Quaker parrot and then, "Kill you both, kill you both. Akkkkkk."

He twisted to the golden cage in the room's corner. "Hush, Typo."

Salty had given him the bird to remind him not to talk to himself, and the joke worked too well. The parrot wouldn't let up. "Hush, Typo. Hush, Typo. Akkkkkk."

The racket stirred Sherlock from his midday slumber. From his spot on the cool kitchen floor, the English bulldog bounded into the living area, jowls shaking, determined to investigate. Watson would have been a good name too, for an ever-loyal dog who sensed when Raspy needed his help, but Sherlock seemed to think Raspy needed him to eat Typo. The dog banged his head against the metal legs supporting Typo's cage, then barked at Typo, who squawked back. Raspy's Saturday afternoon was off to an unproductive start.

After Raspy calmed his pets, he turned his attention back to the text and re-read the words. Was this a sick joke? Or perhaps this was a different joke, a prompt from one of his competitive writer friends to see who could pull off the most outlandish character death—most mystery writers he knew possessed a little gallows humor. But the texter was not in his contacts and the number unknown. He saw dots form on the screen and waited. The new text read:

> By the way, your chances of escaping death aren't good. This author has already killed a podcaster and gotten away with it.

A link followed, and while Raspy knew the danger of clicking on unknown links in text messages, he couldn't help himself. It took him to a newspaper article about a podcaster's death, where the headline "Unsolved Death of Stacy Story" glared at him in red and black. Nothing about Stacy Story's death appeared relevant until Raspy read about the timing. The podcaster died—it said nothing about her being murdered—the day she conducted three author interviews. Raspy realized he'd held his breath when he read the authors' names. They were the same three writers he and Salty planned to interview three days from now for the biggest event of their podcast year.

Raspy clicked on the folder on his computer labeled "Author Episodes," found the sub-folder with the date of the upcoming event, and opened it. Thumbnails of three headshots appeared at the top. He opened and enlarged them side by side. There was William Z. Wisp, the poet; Della Molasses, the romance author; and Edwin Nocturne, the thriller writer. Raspy couldn't imagine being murdered by a poet, especially one who looked like a smug professor, nor a romance author. Though Della dressed to kill in a see-through blouse, he found it hard to believe she'd have much interest in a real killing. And the thin thriller writer with the nervous expression looked like he hadn't been to the gym his whole life. Raspy liked his chances in a fistfight with any of the three. But the threat was murder, not a boxing match.

He looked back at the article and studied it. Stacy Story wasn't well-known in the podcast space. Like Raspy and Salty, she had been a 30-something writer with a day job, a podcast hobbyist who liked to interview authors and help them tell their stories. She was intelligent, with a promising future as a literary fiction writer: a graduate of UC Berkeley and the Iowa Writers' Workshop, and a Pushcart Prize recipient. But why did she die? She—like them—had no criminal record. Her podcast —like theirs—had good ratings on Spotify. And Stacy Story— like Raspy and Salty—had had no prior contact with Wisp, Molasses, or Nocturne before she interviewed them.

Raspy felt sympathy for Stacy Story and a stirring in his gut. If someone like Stacy Story died because she interviewed these authors, was it that difficult to believe that the same fate awaited him and Salty?

He phoned Salty to break the news. On the fourth ring, the call went to voicemail. Raspy texted her instead:

Call me. Now. It's podcast urgent!

TAKE 2

THIS IS LIFE-AND-DEATH SERIOUS

Salty Remarks swallowed the last drop of her draft IPA at the bustling Book End Bar and Grill in NoDa, her and Raspy's artsy-cool neighborhood in Charlotte, North Carolina, which was named for its main street, North Davidson. The brewery was an old favorite for Salty and her boyfriend Josh, who looked pretty fine today in his skinny jeans and tight-fitting T-shirt. She was about to order another round for them when her phone buzzed. It was Raspy. What now?

She and Raspy had been together all morning recording online with two authors and planning for their big year-end live event, and it was Saturday afternoon, time to kick back, have a few drinks, and spend some quality time in the sack with Josh. She ignored the call and gave Josh a smile.

A text followed that included the words *Podcast urgent*. It always felt urgent around Raspy, her best friend since college, so much so that she joked with him that his last name—Fuse—fit his short fuse liable to burn fast from worry. He worried most about doing his job well, whether that be his regular job as a paralegal for a criminal defense firm or this podcast gig. "Podcast urgent" could mean sketching out the entire next season or coming up with a strategy to get an interview with the recent National Book Award winner. Salty ignored the text and motioned to the server.

Her phone buzzed again.

> Where are you?

She turned the phone over, but the buzzing didn't stop. When she flipped the phone back, there were four more texts.

> Put your beer down and call me.

> Take your hands off Josh and call.

> This is serious, Salt.

He'd called her Salt since they'd teamed up. He was the Pepper to her salt, a lame joke about their skin color.

> Life-and-death serious.

Okay, "life-and-death serious" was worth a return call. Raspy had never gone there before. She told Josh she'd be right back, then whispered in his ear what she had in mind for their afternoon, which made him smile.

She stepped onto the bar's deck and called Raspy, who wasted no time unloading the urgent facts.

Salty took a deep breath. She eyed Josh through the window

and tapped the toe of her Converse sneaker. "Sounds like a prank, Raspy. You think one of these authors is going to kill us because we ask hard questions or pick apart their writing process?"

There was a pause on the other end. "That California podcaster's death creeped me out. Don't you think we should report this to the police?"

"Last I recall, you weren't a big fan of the thin blue line, and I'm with you there." She waved at Josh through the window and pointed to her phone. He lifted his Guinness to her, drained it, and went for a refill at the crowded bar. "If we call the police, what are they going to do? Listen to our interviews to see if we can Perry Mason them into confessing?"

She heard Raspy sigh.

"It's Saturday, Raspy. Turn off your computer. Watch *Only Murders in the Building*. Or that PBS British crime series you and Sherlock love. Forget about this joker-texter. We'll talk on Monday."

"You think we should do the three interviews Tuesday night?"

Salty laughed. "Why not? I've never interviewed a killer before." She heard Raspy groan, but it couldn't be helped. They'd spent six months planning this event and too much money they didn't have booking one of the nicest theaters in Charlotte. It would take tremendous luck to fulfill their shared dream of writing and podcasting full time, but this event could be their turning point. And maybe the hype of a few "killer" authors would be what she needed to give up her day job as a freelance ad copy writer. No way she would cancel—they'd worked too hard for this. Besides, she wasn't a believer in authors who plotted murders instead of stories.

On the way back into the bar, she received a text from an unknown number.

> Hello Salty. I presume you've heard from Raspy so I won't repeat what I told him. The reason for this text is to assure you the threat is real. Hope you survive, but live or die, what happens Tuesday night will make a great story. Good luck. As I told Raspy, I am a big fan of your podcast, and truth be told, you're the better writer. Your recent thriller was to die for.

Maybe she needed to reassess this risk.

Salty went into the bar, grabbed Josh by the arm, and pulled him toward the door. She had to relieve some tension. Two hours should be enough time. She texted Raspy in Josh's car.

> Let's meet at the usual spot at 5 to talk about these killer authors.

TAKE 3
PODCAST SUPPORT TEAM THEATRICS

After Raspy received Salty's text about their 5:00 pm meeting, he called Dan Pierce, their twice-as-old-as-them podcast website guru and all-around internet sleuth.

"Got a job for you." Raspy talked while he walked back and forth across the five feet of pacing room he had in his snug apartment, too jittery to sit.

"What? No foreplay."

"This is serious, Dan."

"If it's serious, then it's Dan the IT Man to you."

Raspy hated it when Dan played the nickname card. Dan was always whining about getting paid late and not paid enough—though he set the prices—and said he felt the least Raspy and Salty could do was give him the respect he deserved. It was why Salty told Raspy she wasn't dealing with the guy any longer.

Raspy swallowed his pride. "I have an important job for Dan the IT Man, if he is up to the task."

"You're three months behind on my bills." Dan's voice had an edge to it. "This is not a non-profit enterprise."

Raspy relaxed as he thought about the upside of being murdered. He could stiff Dan. That would give him something to whine about.

"We'll pay you." But as Raspy said it, he made a mental note. This was going to be the last job Dan the IT Man performed for *Under the Covers*. They needed his expertise, but at what cost? He returned calls and texts late, showed irritation with new assignments, and lashed out at them about their deficient WordPress skills, which was supposed to be his area of expertise, not theirs. He brought up non-payment in every conversation, but his tone was more threatening in the last few weeks. As Dan the IT Man said often, he said again now: "I always get paid, one way or the other."

Raspy hated to use the podcast's limited resources for this assignment, but he needed information that was beyond a Google search, and Dan had a knack for finding things from the deepest, darkest corners of the internet. He wasted no time with his instructions, but Dan was all questions.

"What's she to you? Why do you care how she died?"

What to tell? What not to tell? Raspy didn't feel comfortable telling Dan the IT Man someone threatened them with murder. He might not do the job without an advance. "I care because she died the same day she interviewed the three authors we plan to interview on Tuesday. I'd like to know what happened to her."

"Why not just wait until Tuesday?"

"What?"

"To see if you die." Dan had become creepy too.

"Can you do it or not?"

"You'll have my report in a few hours. But remember—"

"I know. You always get paid, one way or the other. Jesus, Dan, this isn't *Godfather IV*."

Raspy ended the call and tossed his phone on his sofa. When it bounced, it lit up. He sat on the sofa, leaned back into the cushions, and picked up the phone to see a text message from their one sponsor:

> Have you thought about the re-negotiation request?

This was the fourth time in two days Mike's Used Bookstore had pushed for a re-negotiation of their one-year sponsorship deal, which still had eight months remaining. Mike Reader, the owner, said the deal was too rich for him now, "since you misrepresented the number of downloads."

They had not misrepresented the downloads because you can't misrepresent something that hasn't happened. They'd offered projections. Mike knew that when he signed on. The podcast needed the money and needed the time to grow, so yes, they'd thought about the request, but no, it would not happen.

Raspy swiped a hand over his chin, then texted back.

> We appreciate the sponsorship and prefer to stick with the original deal. We're working hard. Good things to come.

Seconds later, he had a response.

> I knew you wouldn't agree and have set
> Plan B in motion.

What the heck was Plan B? Raspy did not know, but he didn't have time to worry because he had to arrange the audio team to record the live interviews with their killer authors, a task on his checklist he'd failed to admit to Salty he hadn't completed. He called the audio company they'd worked with and made it past the gatekeeper to the owner.

"My assistant tells me you want my guys for your big event on Tuesday. You've got a lot of nerve, Raspy."

Penny Leverage, the owner of An Earful Studio, had been after him for months to interview her ex-husband, Rocky Fist, saying she'd forgive their four-month unpaid bill for the courtesy, "to get Rocky off my back so he can talk about the book he wrote in prison and not because his book doesn't suck." Rocky Fist's book did suck—they must not teach writing in prison— which was why Raspy had ignored Penny's request.

"Rocky said he wants to be on the podcast?"

"He did. Said he wants to give voice to his written words. Isn't that your motto? Prison must have been boring as hell for him to tune into your show."

Raspy made a quick decision. "We'll put Rocky on the panel too. Just provide the audio team so we can focus on the interviews."

Penny snorted. "Things have changed. I need to get paid too."

"Tell you what. If you throw in your security guard, I'll pay you right after the event." Raspy didn't share that he might be dead when the debt came due.

Penny huffed. "This is the last time you break a promise to me, Raspy. My ex-husband is a lousy author but a good debt collector. Understood?"

Raspy understood that Rocky Fist had gone to jail for attempted murder. Still, an ex-con named Rocky Fist seemed like a good man to have on a panel if a murder broke out.

TAKE 4
THREE MYSTERIOUS WRITERS

"A poem is like a well, and with each reading, the reader can sup but one more crystal drop from its bottomless depths." The poet's eyes were enormous and round, almost glimmering, above the tangle of scarves—two? three? Could that be four scarves?—around his neck.

Salty looked up from the laptop where the YouTube video was playing. "No way this guy murders us."

"According to whoever's texting us, there's a one-in-three chance." Raspy sipped his cappuccino. They were at their usual spot, Books and Beans, settled into a warmly lit corner booth, surrounded by bookshelves.

Salty looked back at the video, watched the poet read his next stanza, and cringed. "If this is the guy, his bad similes will kill us before the interview is over."

"A tip for staying alive, Salt: take death threats more seriously."

Salty stopped the video. "It's more likely this is a joke than a literary murder for hire. If we put this plotline in a story, no reader would believe it."

"Truth is stranger than fiction."

"Point taken." Salty put a check beside the first name on her list. "William Z. Wisp, poet and potential murderer number one. What about the romance author?"

"Right, Della Molasses." Raspy pulled up Della's press information on his computer while Salty swirled her cold brew with oat milk. She leaned in to read over Raspy's shoulder while he read the words on the publicity sheet aloud. "'Della Molasses's heroines play hard for the happy ending—and her hunky heroes will make you hot.'"

Salty laughed. "Well, if William's similes don't kill us, Della's alliteration will."

Raspy skimmed further down the page. "She's put out three salacious romances a year for ten years. Have you read her latest book for the interview?"

"*A Steamy Cup of Cocoa?* Yeah, just finished it last night. Her heroine is a man-slayer of a different kind. It might inspire her to spike our hot chocolate and tie us to a bedpost for her version of a good time, but not kill us."

Salty peered at Della's author photo, all auburn curls and pink lipstick. "What about the thriller writer? I haven't read his book yet."

"Me neither, but I've got it here." Raspy pulled the paperback out of his laptop bag: *Blood on Her Hands* by Edwin Nocturne. He opened the cover with an image of a red handprint and flipped to a random page in the afterword, where he read aloud. "'What many people don't know about strychnine is it doesn't need to be ingested. Simple atmospheric exposure via the nasal membranes is enough to incapacitate the lungs.'"

Raspy jumped as his phone lit up on the table. He picked it up and read the text to himself and then reported to Salty. "Dan the IT Man found the coroner's report on the dead podcaster. She died of respiratory failure." He stared Salty in the eyes. "Still think this is a prank?"

Salty grabbed her phone, dialed a number, and put it on speaker. "It's time we got some answers."

"From whom?"

"From the person who set us up."

TAKE 5

A PODCAST BOOKER MAKES THE CONNECTIONS

Salty's outgoing call rang three times before their problem answered. "It's a smooth decibel day at Your Number One Podcast Booker in the U-S-of-A. This is Barry Bookum listening. What can I book for you today?"

Salty didn't have the stomach for Barry Bookum. He gouged his author clients to put them on podcasts while the podcasters did the work and incurred the costs. They had avoided him in the past and done just fine with their guest list, but he had access to A-list authors through the Big Five publishers—likely nepotism to the highest degree—so when he had pitched Raspy the idea of a three-author panel for their year-end extravaganza, Salty had relented. Now Barry Bookum had some explaining to do.

Salty was ready to launch into a series of rat-a-tat questions when Raspy waved his hands in front of her face and pointed to himself. Despite his short anxiety fuse, Raspy sometimes had a longer fuse when dealing with people. Salty was as loyal as

Sherlock the bulldog was to the people she cared about, but she could also be, well, salty. She conceded with a scowl.

"Barry, this is Raspy Fuse."

It sounded like Barry Bookum flipped through something. Was it paper? No. There were also clicks, like it was an old-school Rolodex. "Raspy, Raspy Fuse. Good to hear your voice. Love the *Under the Covers* podcast. You ready for the big production? My authors are going to kill it."

"That's what I'm afraid of."

"Come again?"

"We have a few questions about your three authors."

"We?"

"Sorry. Salty Remarks is on the phone with us."

Silence. Perhaps Barry Bookum knew Salty didn't care much for him. Or maybe he knew something about their murderous situation. Whatever the reason, the number one podcast booker in the U-S-of-A recovered fast.

"Hello, Salty. Loved your latest thriller. You're going to hit it off with Edwin Nocturne."

Salty wondered if Barry the Blowhard—the name she'd given him—knew what they were facing. After all, another podcaster had died because one of Barry's three authors had a knack for murder. "About Edwin Nocturne?" she asked. "Is *Blood on Her Hands* an autobiography?"

Barry Bookum gave off a belly laugh that sounded like someone stepped on a goose. "Good one, Salty. It's a killer book for sure, but he's not a she, or a killer. It's a thriller. All the rage."

Salty sat back and folded her arms and Raspy jumped in. He held the microphone close to be heard over the background chatter of the coffee shop. "Barry, we're trying to get a profile on our guests before the interview to know how they might react to our questions. You know, the things you can't find online. Since you mentioned Edwin first, is there anything you can tell us about him? Anything unusual?"

"Like what?"

Salty whispered the words, "Is he a crazy killer?" Raspy mouthed back, "Careful," and leaned into the phone. "We once had a situation with an unstable author. Can't be too careful these days." Raspy pretended to laugh.

"My authors are not unstable. I'm the number one podcast booker in the U-S-of-A."

Even Raspy was losing his patience. "Barry, we already work with you. We don't need the sales pitch. If you have information that one of your clients might be dangerous and you conceal that information from us, I don't think a prosecutor will care how good a podcast booker you are."

"Well. I see. That is…a pertinent point." There were more shuffles on Barry's end. "Ah, here we go. Got his file right here. Yes. Uh-huh. I shouldn't tell you this, what with medical privacy rights and all, but Edwin had a nervous breakdown last year and spent a few months in the hospital. But he came back strong with his recent bestseller and his doctor has cleared him to go on tour! He shouldn't be a problem."

Salty drew a question mark in the air and Raspy followed up. Barry told them what Salty suspected. "Edwin's breakdown had to do with that podcaster in California who died the day she interviewed him. The rags wrote conspiracy stories about it and tried to frame him for the murder after *Blood on Her Hands* came out. Some called the book a confession. It was nothing of the sort. Edwin liked the podcaster."

Salty grabbed the phone and talked into the speaker. "Barry, with this being his first interview after his breakdown, listeners will expect us to ask about the connections between Edwin's book and that podcaster's death. How do you think he'll react?"

"Won't tell you how to do your job, Salty, but I advise caution. Good news is Edwin has a therapist who has helped him. In fact, she's also helped the other two authors who were there."

This time, Raspy drew a question mark in the air and Salty responded with a question to Barry. "By them, do you mean William Z. Wisp and Della Molasses, the other authors you booked on our show with Edwin, and by there, do you mean the interview with the dead podcaster?"

Barry Bookum honked again. "Nothing gets by you, Salty."

Salty gritted her teeth, closed her eyes, and thought of things that soothed her. Time with Josh. Baby wallabies. Banana splits. "Barry. Our question is: Should we be worried about these authors?"

"William's a poet. I'd only be worried about him if you don't like poetry. Same is true with Della, assuming romance is not your thing."

"Why are they seeing the same therapist?"

"Same problem as Edwin. They felt terrible about that podcaster's death. And they felt even worse—more like depressed—when the true crime bloggers mentioned their connection with the case. Guess the doc specializes in writer trauma."

Salty tossed the phone to Raspy and exhaled. Raspy took his time with the pace of the next question. "What made you book them together again on the same podcast at the same time?"

"You told me you needed a big audience. Think of the hype, baby. The suspense. The drama. You'll kill it in the ratings."

"But—"

"Come on Raspy. Lightning doesn't strike twice in the same place. Plus, they've all got local connections. A support team, if you will."

Raspy said he didn't understand.

"Edwin has been working with a local web designer named Dan something-or-other who he respects. He plans to connect with him when he's in town to do your interview."

Raspy almost upset his cappuccino as he covered the phone and mouthed to Salty, "Dan the IT Man."

"And Della Molasses appears to be in love. Ever the romantic. She met somebody online named Mike Reader who runs a local bookstore near you."

Before Raspy could react, Salty waved him off. "What about William Wisp?" she quipped. "Did he fall in love with a local poet?"

"No. No. No. He turned his latest poetry book into an audiobook and struck a deal with an outfit called An Earful Studio. His contact is Penny something-or-other."

"Penny Leverage."

"Oh, you know her? Well, that's all I know."

Salty's voice became firm. "Not quite, Barry. Tell us the name of the therapist."

"Not sure I can do that."

Salty said loud enough for Barry to hear. "Raspy, if we cancel these interviews, does Barry get paid?"

"Hold on, now. No need to cancel interviews. I suppose

there's no harm in sharing the name of the therapist as long as you didn't hear it from me."

Salty wrote the therapist's name on a napkin, ended the call with Barry, and turned to Raspy. "Any developments in our relationships with Dan, Mike, and Penny? Anything I should know?"

Raspy stood and talk-walked by their booth. "Dan and Penny are upset about our past due bills. Dan reminded me he always gets paid one way or the other and Penny says she'll sic her ex-convict ex-husband on us if we don't pay her. As for Mike, he said something about a Plan B because we wouldn't renegotiate our sponsorship deal. I don't see how any of their gripes explain their connections to these authors."

Salty digested what Raspy told her. "Dan and Penny don't benefit from our death. If we die, they don't get paid, so Dan's connection to Edwin Nocturne and Penny's connection to William Wisp don't appear to be some murder-for-hire scheme. Mike, however, owes us money, so if we go away, so does his obligation."

Raspy shook his head. "You're suggesting that Mike Reader's Plan B to end our sponsorship deal is to have Della Molasses end us? First, do you know how crazy that sounds? It's only $3,500 for the annual sponsorship. Second, what's in it for Della Molasses? And third, how is a romance writer going to kill us? Smother us with kisses?"

"Sit down, Raspy. You're making me jumpy."

"I'm making you jumpy? Not the fact we're outnumbered six to two and have no idea what's coming?" Raspy rejoined her in the booth.

Salty tapped the name Della Molasses on her list and

drained the last of her cold brew. "Maybe Mike found out that Della Molasses killed the other podcaster, and he's blackmailing her to help him."

"Mike Reader is the owner of a used bookstore. Not a detective. I think you're wrong. And we shouldn't assume our people contacted these authors. What if it was the other way around?"

Raspy had a point. The three people who knew the most about their podcasting business besides them were Dan the IT Man, Mike Reader, and Penny Leverage. They had special access to the Tuesday event, and they knew how, where, and when to find Salty and Raspy before and during the show. Dan had access to their website, including their emails. Penny controlled the audio crew and security guard. And Mike was in charge of publicity and admission to the event. If one of these authors wanted to kill them, establishing a relationship with one of their team members would be helpful. The questions were who and why?

Raspy's sigh broke Salty's train of thought. "I don't know, Salt. There are a lot of coincidences here, a lot of unknowns. Wouldn't it be safer to cancel the live show?"

"Sure. It also would have been safer never to have podcasted. Never to have written. Never to have taken any risks. When have you and I ever gone for safer, Raspy?"

Raspy smiled. "You know us too well."

"Well enough to know that if we cancel, we'll wonder whether any of this was real, and whether one of these authors is going to jump out of the bushes someday and stab us with a fountain pen. I'd rather investigate and I know you would too. You're a mystery writer. I'm a thriller writer. Let's reverse engineer their plot."

Raspy laughed. "You had me at 'stab us with a fountain pen.'" He picked up Salty's note with the therapist's name Barry Bookum gave them. He read the name aloud. "Doctor Speak Toomey? Really?"

Salty snapped the laptop lid shut. "I've got a headache. It's time to call the doctor."

TAKE 6

THERAPY COMES IN THREES

Doctor Speak Toomey's Manhattan office walls were painted with bright preschool-like colors, part of what offered a welcoming, feel-good environment for her psychology practice. But what her author patients—and the psychologist herself—found even more comforting were the overflowing, wall-to-wall bookshelves in every room.

Doctor Toomey was about to hold a group therapy session for three patients she'd been treating separately for the past year. The idea came to her when she confirmed they were going to appear together on the *Under the Covers* podcast. The last time these writers had appeared together on a podcast, their interviewer died and their connection to the podcaster's death turned their lives upside down. This might be the most important therapy session of her career.

Doctor Toomey's path to this session had been twenty years in the making. In college, she'd majored in creative writing to achieve her dream of being a successful author, but when her professors told her she didn't have what it took—"You're not that good a writer," they said—she went where her parents always wanted her to go, into medicine.

Toomey avoided dwelling in the dark basement of her shattered dream by throwing herself into her medical career instead. In her spare time, the writer hidden deep in her soul drew her to libraries and bookstores, where she read and scribbled, and where she met writers and listened to their complaints. Some of them became clients, and those clients referred her to their writer friends. When she realized she had built a reputation in New York as the writer's therapist—and that helping authors navigate the ups and downs along the road to literary success was *almost* as fulfilling as walking that road herself—she committed to her newfound calling and set up a practice devoted to writers. It did not surprise her how quickly her client list grew. If she'd learned nothing else, she knew that being a writer was 99 percent head-game.

The three authors would arrive in less than thirty minutes, giving Doctor Toomey just enough time to study their files again before their session. Rather than turning to her computer, she read through the pages in three manila folders. She preferred working with the hard copies—despite the clutter they made on her desk—for the same reason she preferred the smell and feel of the bound pages of a book to an e-reader.

Her records reminded her that Edwin Nocturne, Della Molasses, and William Z. Wisp were similar in two ways but different in others. One thing they had in common was the inciting incident that led them to her: what she liked to call death by podcasting. The other was their desire for literary success, which they defined as commercial success, meaning lots of books sold and many adoring fans. It hadn't happened for them—"yet," they liked to point out—but their media attention in the last year had given them enough visibility to make them worthwhile guests on any literary podcast and to keep them hoping for more. And yet, why William Z. Wisp thought he had a chance for financial success as a writer was beyond Doctor Toomey. He was a poet, after all. The other two authors wrote romance and thrillers, crowded fields to be sure, but also fields where the top players made big bucks.

Doctor Toomey tapped Della Molasses's folder as she thought about the differences in her three clients. Della had struggled as a romance author. Her first book found an agent and a large publisher, but when she presented her manuscript for book two, the publisher passed and it forced her to go the indie route. During this phase of her writing journey, she delved into more spicy erotica, and while many romance authors find financial success publishing their own books in this genre, Della didn't. She became bitter, envious of other authors' success, including that of her writer friends. Underneath her saccharine surface, she was what Doctor Toomey might describe in non-clinical terms as "bat shit crazy."

William Z. Wisp developed a troubled writer's soul for other reasons. He never sold many poetry chapbooks, but he didn't blame the writing. His villain was the reading public, who he called "uneducated dullards" because they didn't consume poetry at the rate they read romance and thrillers. Putting him in the same room with Della and Edwin would test Doctor Toomey's abilities. In their last session, William lashed out at her because the poetry section of her book collection occupied less than one shelf. She pointed out that poetry books were thinner, but he ignored her. Not only did he crave attention for his work, he demanded it.

Thriller writer Edwin Nocturne had the most interesting recent development in his writing career and was much closer to achieving financial success than Della and William. A reputable publisher backed his latest book, *Blood on Her Hands*, and spent big dollars to promote it. His problem—or maybe it wasn't a problem if terrible publicity is good publicity—was that the internet bloggers tagged him the primary suspect in the California podcaster's death that was the inspiration for his book. He was quick to defend himself in their therapy sessions, saying he'd developed a theory about what happened to the podcaster because he was one of the last three people to see her alive and had used that theory to write his thriller, a work of fiction. Critics had called Edwin an opportunistic voyeur who wrote an interesting book, a combination sure to lead to sales from curious readers.

Doctor Toomey had used her individual sessions with each author to uncover their feelings about the dead podcaster, the link that tied them together. Edwin claimed he was heartbroken and just had to write about her. His decision seemed to pay off. William expressed remorse, an odd reaction to the woman's death, and wrote an unpublished poem about the tragedy he'd refused to share during his sessions. Della tried to forget the death ever happened, though she displayed a hint of jealousy at how Edwin had turned the debacle into a bestseller, and seemed offended that she had not been the center of the dead podcaster's attention. She recounted that when the woman interviewed her, she had read none of Della's books and dismissed romance writing. She referred to Della's books as "chick lit," a fact Della had reported to Doctor Toomey with shoulders drawn back.

The front door chime let Doctor Toomey know one of her patients had arrived. Five minutes later, everyone sat in the conference room for the therapy session that she sensed would change somebody's career. Della twiddled the clasp on her alligator-skin purse. Edwin, who sat next to Della on the couch, rubbed the knuckles of his long, pale hands. William sat erect in a chair far away from Della and Edwin.

Doctor Toomey started with a courtesy. "Can I offer everyone something to drink?"

They said "No," "No thank you," and "Nothing for me." They all looked straight ahead and refused to acknowledge each other.

"Okay then. Let's get started."

Doctor Toomey began with the preliminaries, including "the need to be honest with yourselves and with each other," and she expressed her gratitude for their willingness to put in the work today. But when their faces remained frozen and their postures stiff, she hit them where it counted. "Unless you come to terms about your shared past, your appearance on the *Under the Covers* podcast will be a disaster. It won't help your book sales and will hurt your careers."

William Z. Wisp looked like he was trying to maintain his icy expression, but color rose in his cheeks. When he spoke, his voice had lost its usual ethereal lilt. "I find it distasteful to be here with these people. What they do is not literature."

Della Molasses rolled her eyes, and Edwin Nocturne

coughed. Doctor Toomey smiled. "William, do you think what you said is constructive?"

"You said to be honest. I am just stating a fact."

"It's more like an opinion, William."

William lifted his head. "To which I am entitled."

Doctor Toomey smiled again. "Yes, William. You are entitled to your opinion. However, that does not mean you have to express it when it might hurt other people's feelings." Doctor Toomey thought it appropriate her office had preschool-friendly colors, because she sometimes felt like she was talking to toddlers. "You agreed to appear with Della and Edwin on the upcoming podcast, after all."

"The podcast is nothing more than a publicity stunt by that booker. He hopes the show will devolve into a train-wreck discussion about the connection between Edwin's so-called 'book' and Stacy Story's death, and he will get the credit for booking a show that goes viral."

"It's good for you to say her name," Doctor Toomey said. "Stacy Story's death is something we've discussed but not as a group. Perhaps we should start there."

Della raised her hand. "Doctor, as you know, I've seen and written about a lot of big dicks, but I've never encountered a dick as large as William Z. Wisp, either in fact or fiction, and it is frightful." Della batted her lashes at William. "On the plus side, William has a point about Edwin, an evil man who seeks to profit by Stacy Story's death."

Edwin Nocturne glared at Della Molasses. "You're jealous because nobody cares about the porn you write."

"That's rich, coming from someone who writes fear-porn," Della shot back. "And by the way, people love porn."

Doctor Toomey asked for calm. "Please everyone. You're all professional writers. No one genre is better than another. Just different. Don't compare yourselves. You have your own voices and your own writing journeys."

"Except," Della said, "Edwin's journey includes a book that suggests a female writer killed Stacy and everyone knows there was one female writer she interviewed that day. Me. So thank you very much, Edwin. I'm billing you for every book sale I lose because of the conspiracy theory you created."

"I agree," William said. "Interviewers care less about my poems than what happened to Stacy Story and what part I may have had in her death. When was the last time anybody asked me about the musicality of my enjambment?"

Doctor Toomey had heard the story of Stacy Story's death from her three clients' points of view, but pieces were missing and *Blood on Her Hands* left out details Edwin Nocturne shared with her that could implicate him. Her clients had met separately with Stacy after the episode and before she died to voice their complaints. They were jealous of the attention given to the others and upset with the tone and substance of Stacy's questions. None of that was a reason to kill someone. And yet, it didn't help that they'd all been dealing with financial issues and self-doubts, and they were on the verge of giving up when the podcast didn't go well for them.

Della Molasses voiced what Doctor Toomey was thinking. "One of us poisoned Stacy Story. The question is who and why."

"Della. It was you," Edwin said. "I didn't name you as the killer to avoid costly litigation. You're envious of every published author and the fact that Stacy didn't put you on a pedestal and throw roses at your feet infuriated you."

"Nice try, Edwin," William said. "Suggesting a female writer did it was a red herring. You were working on a thriller about a murdered podcaster before Stacy died and you ensured the storyline intersected with her death."

Doctor Toomey watched this exchange with interest. She waited for Della to share her theory about who killed Stacy Story and Della didn't disappoint. In fact, she did it in rhyme. "Edwin and William did cut them a deal, and the poison they used was really quite real." Della stood and curtsied to William when she finished and Doctor Toomey smiled to herself. This was working out better than expected. These people were real characters. It was time to redirect the conversation.

"It appears everyone agrees that someone in this room killed Stacy Story. Is it a good idea for you to go on another podcast together?"

Della's face brightened. "I can't wait to see how William and Edwin kill again. I bet they have a sequel in the works."

"Preposterous," William said. "I have no desire to hurt anyone, except to cut them with the truth of my verse."

"Except you do, William. You do." Della beamed. "You want to hurt every creature in the universe who doesn't like or understand your poetry. Tell you what I'll do. In my next book, I'll include a scene where one character reads one of your poems to another and she gets so excited, she strips down and makes love to him on a bus, holding the poem in the air, so every passenger can see your name, except, William, you know where they will be looking."

William stood and addressed Doctor Toomey. "I can't be in the same room with these sentence slingers any longer. I will be at the podcast event but only because I am committed by contract and because I paid that booker a hefty fee."

When the conference room door slammed behind William, Della leaned toward Edwin Nocturne and whispered in his ear. "What will you pay me to screw those podcasters to death for you?"

Edwin left the room without responding and Della smiled at the doctor as she followed him out. Doctor Toomey looked at her notes. She hadn't felt this excited since the day she went to college to become a writer.

TAKE 7

HAVE RECORDERS, WILL INVESTIGATE

On their Monday drive to New York City to see Doctor Toomey in Salty's beat-up Jeep Wrangler that her mom handed down to her when she graduated college, the two podcasters had time to reflect. It had been twenty-four hours since they'd spoken with Barry Bookum and while their investigation during that time had taught them a lot, there were unanswered questions.

They'd called Doctor Toomey, who surprised them by her willingness to talk about her three patients, but only in person, she said. She wasn't available until tonight, which had given them Sunday to investigate the locals. With audio recorders in hand, they had approached Dan the IT Man, Mike Reader of Mike's Used Bookstore, and Penny Leverage of An Earful Studio to find out what they could about their relationships with the three authors.

While Salty drove, billboards and endless stretches of trees whizzed past on I-85, and Raspy fiddled with his and Salty's audio recorders in his lap. "Where do you want to start?"

Salty opted for the poet's connection to An Earful Studio. "Was Penny Leverage suspicious when you approached her?"

"If she was, she was a talented actor." Raspy hit the fast-forward button and watched the counter until he stopped the recorder. "This is where I asked Penny how she knew William Z. Wisp." He pressed play.

"—read some of his poetry and adored it. I reached out to him on his website to see if I could get autographed copies of his latest book."

"Did Wisp respond?"

"He did. It was exciting."

"Did he tell you Salty and I were going to interview him?"

"Yes. I invited him to do a reading at Mike's Used Bookstore after the show."

"What?"

"He said he'd be delighted. Mike asked your other two panelists to do the same. Only one of them said yes. I believe it was the thriller writer."

Raspy stopped the recorder and Salty kept her eyes on the road as she asked the question. "She didn't say William Wisp reached out to her to turn his poetry into audiobooks?"

"Nope. I asked. She said the idea was a good one but it never came up."

Salty hit the gas and passed a slow car. In driving, and in life, she didn't like to waste time. "Why would William Wisp lie to Barry Bookum about how he connected with Penny Leverage?"

"That question assumes he's the one who lied," Raspy said.

"You don't trust Penny Leverage?"

"Never have trusted her except to provide us with good audio technicians."

Salty had an uneasy feeling in her stomach. "There is something you need to know, Raspy." Salty noticed she was running twenty miles over the speed limit. Too fast, even for her. She backed off the gas. "The first thing Mike did when I saw him yesterday was invite us to the bookstore after our event."

"Did he mention William Wisp and Edwin Nocturne doing a reading?"

"That's just it. He never mentioned it. He said he wanted to drink a few beers with us and make a fresh start."

Salty thought about the side of town where Mike's bookstore was located. She loved a good hole-in-the-wall tattoo parlor or dive bar, but even for her, the bookstore's neighborhood wasn't the best place to be late at night.

They rode in silence for a few minutes until Raspy asked about Della. "What did Mike say about Della reaching out and falling in love with him on the internet?"

"I think we discussed it around the five-minute mark."

Raspy picked up Salty's digital recorder, found the spot, and pushed play. They heard Mike laugh before he said, "—not true. I was the one who reached out to Della four months ago. I thought her profile on the Killer Bee dating app was hot, and with her being an erotic writer and me being a bookstore owner, I thought I might have a chance. She blew me off. Never responded until a few days ago."

"What did she want?"

"She'd found out I was your sponsor, said she was going to

be on the show for the big event, and she wanted some background information on you and Raspy."

"What did you tell her?"

"Everything I knew. Sorry if I did anything wrong, but you guys are an open book with what you put on your website and say on your podcast. I thought if I cooperated with her, she might change her mind about me. I was right. She was very appreciative."

"Was there anything unusual she wanted to know about Raspy and me?"

There was a delay in Mike's response. "Come to think of it, there was. She asked if you guys were married, in serious relationships, or had any children. When I told her 'No,' she said, 'That's good.' I don't know why it mattered, unless maybe she's bisexual and thinks you guys are hot." Mike laughed and Raspy stopped the recording.

Either Della Molasses hoped for a podcast-themed threesome with Salty and Raspy—which intrigued Salty but wasn't that plausible—or Della wanted to avoid collateral damage when she killed them. And yet, she wasn't the one who was going to surprise them at the bookstore after the show. That privilege fell to the poet and the thriller writer, thanks to Mike Reader and Penny Leverage cooperating together. But why, if Penny Leverage was being honest about the readings after the show, would Della Molasses decline Mike's invitation to read at Mike's store? Had Mike really invited her? Salty smoothed back her ponytail, as if that would somehow help calm her swimming brain. "How did it go with Dan the IT Man?"

"The IT man is a broken record. He harped on when we

were going to pay him. Did his Godfather 'I always get paid' shtick again."

"What did he say about Edwin Nocturne?"

"It's the one connection where the stories match up. He said Nocturne reached out to him about updating his website."

"Really? A New York-based author reached out to a small-time web designer in North Carolina. A little too coincidental, don't you think?"

"I do." Raspy found the spot in his recording and pushed the play button. Salty heard Raspy's voice first.

"How did Edwin Nocturne find you?"

"I'm Dan the IT Man. Everyone finds me sooner or later."

"No offense, Dan, but you're not the only guy who works on websites."

"Edwin said he liked the website I did for you. He was insistent I help him. Even paid me a retainer up front of $5,000. Imagine that, Raspy, a client who pays for my work."

"I said you'd get paid, Dan. Did he ask you questions about Salty and me after he promised to send you $5,000?"

"How much time do you have?"

Raspy pushed the stop button and Salty could feel his eyes on her while she kept her eyes on the road. Her curiosity got to her. "Well?"

Raspy took a deep breath. "Dan took great pleasure when he shared with me all the things he told Edwin. To hear Dan tell it, Edwin was very curious about you and me. How we approach our interviews. Our habits. Our strengths. Our weaknesses. Where we live. What we like to eat. Our favorite beverages. You name it, Edwin wanted to know the answers."

"And did Dan give him answers?"

Raspy nodded. "Not only did he give him answers, he provided him with screenshots from the internet of where we live, the coffee shops and bars we frequent, where we work out, where we record, and even the branch bank where we do business."

"Did you—"

"Damn right I did." Raspy clenched his fists. "I let him have it. But he just smiled, handed me a note, and said 'Tick-Tock' before pointing me to the door."

"A note?"

Raspy reached in his pocket. "Have it right here. It says: 'Pay me everything you owe me plus 20 percent interest or I will continue to help Edwin Nocturne.'"

Salty tightened her fingers on the wheel. "I hate to give in to blackmail, but we owe him money. Maybe we should pay him today and be done. One less murderous helper to watch out for tomorrow night."

"Dan's lying. His smirk when he handed me the note told me he'll help Edwin even if we pay him. Because—and this is the way the guy thinks—he knows that if we get knocked off, he can exploit our intellectual property for financial gain, and he believes he can take over the podcast and turn a profit more quickly than we have."

Author murderers with accomplices now seemed a less far-fetched fantasy, and as the Manhattan skyscrapers crept into view under a late afternoon sun, Salty felt the fatigue of what they'd been through and what lay ahead. They'd driven ten hours one way, and they faced the same long drive back tomorrow. She was tired physically but also tired of the misdirection and run-around. Before they returned to their hometown lion's den, it was time they got some answers from New York's finest writer therapist.

They parked in the underground lot, found their way to the lobby, and rode the elevator to the 53rd floor. When they exited into the hallway, Salty pointed at the sign that read: Author Rewrite Therapy Services. "I wonder if she's taking new clients."

They opened the office door, and a chime announced their presence for their after-hours meeting. The receptionist desk was unoccupied, but they didn't have to wait long for a woman in her early 40s to appear through an inner door. "You must be Salty Remarks and Raspy Fuse. Welcome." She extended her hand and shook, first with Salty, and then with Raspy. "I'm Doctor Speak Toomey. I bet you're tired after your trip. Please come into my conference room and have a seat."

The pizza smell grabbed Salty's attention when they entered the conference room.

"I figured you'd be starving from your long drive so I ordered from a local pizzeria. They make the best hand-tossed pizza in New York. Help yourself." She pointed at the credenza. "There's water too."

Salty hadn't realized how hungry she was—and hangry. Her potential murder didn't seem quite so bad with a good slice of pizza in front of her.

Everyone filled their plates, sat at the conference room table, and made small talk while they ate. Raspy mentioned the doctor's bookshelves that lined the four walls. "You must be a voracious reader. Do you have a favorite genre?"

The doctor smiled as she finished chewing. "As long as it's a compelling story, I don't care about the genre, but in recent years, I've enjoyed reading true crime." She dabbed at her mouth with a napkin. "Do either of you know the name of the first true crime book?"

Salty thought back to her college class on contemporary novels. Those books had appealed to her way more than the dusty Victorians. "Was it Truman Capote's *In Cold Blood*, about the 1950s murder of a family in Kansas?"

"That's a good guess. It was Capote's writing style, with research help from Harper Lee, that made critics, librarians, and readers realize for the first time how engaging true crime stories could be. Up to that point, the writers were cops, prosecutors, judges, and newspaper reporters."

"What was the first true crime book?" Raspy asked.

"A book of essays in the 1920s that included a story on Lizzie Borden, the accused but acquitted suspect in the most famous unsolved ax murder of the 1890s." The doctor laughed. "But I put my money on the Bible. Lots of killing in that book. Assuming it's true, of course."

Salty smiled to herself. The good doctor had a sense of humor, which was interesting given what Raspy had dug up on her past. "I understand you wanted to be a writer when you were younger?"

The simple question extinguished the glow in Doctor Toomey's cheeks, and it took her a moment to recover. "We all choose majors in college that don't pan out. Dreams don't pay the bills, do they?" She laughed, but Salty could tell she forced it. Perhaps a little encouragement might help.

"Writing and publishing a book doesn't have to be an all-or-nothing proposition. Many published authors we interview have day jobs to pay the bills." Salty shifted into interview mode, as if she were asking an author about their writing life. "If you could write any kind of book you wanted to write in your spare time, what kind would it be?"

"Engaging with my clients is a full-time job with no spare time to write books. But enough about me." The doctor reached out, collected the paper plates, and walked them to the trash can in the corner. When she returned, she said, "Let's talk about why you made this trip."

Raspy folded his hands in his lap. "We're concerned about our live interviews tomorrow night with Della Molasses, Edwin Nocturne, and William Wisp."

"Concerned how?"

Salty was more direct. "The rumors are one of them killed a podcaster."

"I know about the rumors and I've talked with my clients about them. I can't tell you what they told me due to doctor-patient confidentiality rules."

"We've read their denials." Salty tapped her toe against her chair. "Hardly comforting."

"And why is that?" Doctor Toomey sounded curious.

"Because we received an anonymous text saying one of them plans to kill us tomorrow night."

"Do you have a dollar bill?" the doctor asked. "I need one from each of you."

Salty and Raspy pulled dollar bills from their wallets and slid them across the table.

"Good," Doctor Toomey said. "You're now my clients. I can advise you."

Salty was quick with the question. "Should we be worried?"

"Yes."

Salty and Raspy looked at one another. Doctor Toomey didn't elaborate.

"Can you tell us why?" Raspy asked.

"Not precisely."

The yes-or-no questions were getting them nowhere, and they were running out of time. Salty called the question. "Tell us who plans to kill us: Della, William, or Edwin?"

Doctor Toomey leaned back in her chair and looked around the room until her eyes zeroed in on a book. She fetched it, dropped it on the table between Salty and Raspy, and tapped the cover. It was *Blood on Her Hands* by Edwin Nocturne.

"Edwin Nocturne plans to kill us?" Salty said.

"I didn't say that."

"What are you saying then?" Raspy asked.

"I am saying I think a crime is about to be committed, but I don't have the direct evidence—a statement of intention to do so by my client—to report it to the authorities. I can't say anything that violates my oath. When I point to this book—" She tapped the cover again. "I'm pointing to a motive, not a person."

Salty now suspected what they were up against. "You think someone—hypothetically—intends to murder us so they can write a book about it, like the internet says Edwin did with Stacy Story?"

"Not a thriller," the doctor said. "More like what I like to read these days—hypothetically speaking."

"True crime?" Raspy asked.

Doctor Toomey shrugged. "You said it, not me."

"Aren't there laws that prohibit murderers from profiting from books they write about crimes they commit?" Salty asked.

"They're called Son of Sam laws." They enacted the first one in New York, Doctor Toomey explained, after serial killer David Berkowitz, also known by his alter ego Son of Sam, sold the publication rights to his salacious story. "But the law was too broad, and the courts struck it down on First Amendment grounds. That's why most Son of Sam laws don't prohibit publication, only the receipt of profits."

Raspy asked what Salty was thinking. "Does that mean one of these authors intends to kill us, even if they go to prison and receive only the fame from writing a true crime bestseller?"

It looked like Doctor Toomey nodded in the affirmative, but Salty couldn't tell for sure.

Raspy's voice shook. "Which one of your clients is that damn crazy?"

"I can't say. I've been treating them for a long time without much progress."

The lack of straight answers frustrated Salty, but she wasn't giving up just yet. Her gut told her to circle back to an earlier topic. "You never answered my question about your own writing dream, Doctor."

Again, the doctor didn't answer. Instead, she rolled her chair toward a bookshelf where she grabbed a liquor bottle and three glasses. "This is a bottle of Writers' Tears. It's Irish whiskey that should be in every author's collection. What writer doesn't have their share of tears?" She poured the caramel-colored liquid into tiny glasses for Salty, Raspy, and herself, and then sniffed the lip of her glass. "Ask your question."

"If you could find the time, what kind of book would you want to write?"

Doctor Toomey raised her glass in Salty's direction and said, "True crime, of course." Maybe it was the whiskey, but the glow was back in the doctor's cheeks.

TAKE 8

SUPPORT TEAM AND AUTHORS UNITE

Dan the IT Man settled in his seat in the far corner of the Meat and Two Sides restaurant, with his back to the wall and his eyes on the entire room, the way he liked it. The folks who dined here didn't seek the avocado toast, smoothies, and acai bowls so popular in NoDa cafes. They, like him, enjoyed their hamburgers rare, their chicken fried to a crisp, and banana pudding as a side. He popped open his laptop, logged into the app that allowed him to send and receive secure messages, and checked the thread. The latest message read:

> Edwin is becoming more insecure by the hour. Assure him that all will go well and his endgame is solid.

Edwin Nocturne entered the restaurant and looked around the faux wood-paneled room. Dan stood, raised his hand, and motioned to Edwin to join him. When the author sat, his hands shook, not a good sign with the podcast event just six hours away. Dan wondered if Edwin would succeed.

Dan had gotten involved to ensure he got paid by Raspy and Salty, but when he heard more about the plan and what Edwin stood to gain, he got greedy. And why not? He'd paid his dues. Why couldn't he make some serious money? Millennials and Gen Z-ers claimed they knew everything about tech, yet they still came running to him when it was time to get some real—or dirty—work done, and the pay was crap. Without him, the *Under the Covers* show would have no website or social media platforms, no followers, and no email list. Worst-case scenario, he'd get paid what they owed him. Best-case scenario, he'd make a fortune and take possession of everything valuable he'd built for *Under the Covers*.

"You okay?" Dan asked. "Why don't you have a drink?"

Edwin picked up the water glass waiting on the table for him and sipped. He opened his mouth to speak, but the server interrupted him to take their order. Edwin shook his head; said he wasn't hungry.

Dan wasn't having it. The man needed his strength. "We'll each have the cube steak with a side of fries and peach cobbler."

When the server left, Edwin looked around as if someone might watch him. "I have to ask you to do something," he whispered.

"That's why I'm here."

"Can you get a seven-inch cold steel throwing knife into the event hall tonight?"

Dan wasn't keen on having a direct part in the havoc Edwin had planned, but he had two good reasons to proceed: the recent message to *assure Edwin that all will go well* and Edwin's promise to share the proceeds of his next book, which was sure to be a bestseller.

"Not a problem," Dan said. "Security will be tight, but as tech support for the podcast, I won't be subject to the same checks as the audience." Dan paused for a few seconds. "I'll hide the knife in a case marked 'IT equipment.' It'll be onstage next to where you sit."

Edwin looked at his hands. "It's not what you think. I may have a dark imagination, but that's not a crime. No one's ever accused Stephen King of murder."

"Not my job to think. My job is to make sure everything goes the way you want it."

"What I mean is I need the knife because William Wisp is crazy enough to kill the podcasters and I mean to stop him."

"I believe you." Dan didn't believe him, but he didn't need to. All he needed to do was make Edwin comfortable. It didn't matter to him who killed Raspy and Salty, or what Stephen King or any other scribbler did in his spare time. From what he'd learned on the internet, you didn't have to be the one who committed the crime to write a bestselling true crime story. Edwin Nocturne would be the perfect one to write the book, and if he was the saint and not the sinner, the publicity angle would be solid.

"Do you think anyone knows why you're helping me?"

"Not a clue. Your cover story is solid." Except it wasn't. One person knew everything.

Their food arrived and Dan took a bite of a French fry. "You need to eat too," he said to Edwin. "Big night ahead of you."

As they ate, Edwin thanked Dan for the help he'd provided.

"The detailed personal information about Salty and Raspy will add color to the book."

Blood red, Dan thought, but he didn't say it.

Dan had to consider how to answer Edwin's next question. "Did you text Raspy and Salty to warn them one of us might kill them?"

Dan gambled on what Edwin wanted to hear. "I did."

"Good. If they're careful, they'll be on their guard, and William Z. Wisp will only bore them with his poetry, not put them in their graves."

Dan didn't care who put Raspy and Salty in their graves.

Mike told his bookseller a woman would arrive for a meeting at 1:30 and to show her back when she got there. "Her name is Della Molasses."

The boy with a slash of purple in his hair nodded with a look that said "whatever," which was typical of the high school help Mike hired one week who got bored and left the next. Mike shrugged before he passed down the narrow aisle bracketed by tall bookshelves on both sides. The last one on the right before his office was the murder mystery section. He touched the shelf and smiled.

It wasn't long before Mike heard a woman's high-pitched laugh at the front of the store. A moment later, there was a rap on the office door. "Hope you're not decent?"

Mike opened the door to the wide-open arms of the sexiest romance author he'd ever met. He hadn't met that many. But still. She grabbed him by the shoulders and gave him a kiss, making him feel like he'd made the right decision to help her. Especially when she pulled him in to her heaving bosoms.

The office was used bookstore utilitarian, with a metal desk, ten-year-old desktop computer that worked now and then, two metal file cabinets, and an upholstered love seat that had seen better days. Della plopped on the love seat and patted the open cushion beside her. "Sit, sit. We have much to discuss."

When Mike sat, Della reached down in her tote bag and pulled out what she called "my love boat trilogy" and handed the books to Mike. "They're autographed."

He looked at the title page and saw she'd written, "To Mike, my most interesting hook-up ever." Mike blushed. When Della first called him, she'd said she had a proposition "for the handsome Mike Reader, owner of Mike's Used Bookstore and sponsor of the *Under the Covers* podcast." While she rambled on about the podcast and her upcoming appearance on the show, Mike looked her up online. His screen flashed him the home page of the flirty romance author's website, complete with titillating book covers and selected quotes like *the softer her voice was in his ear, the harder it was for him to handle.* "I'd like to hire you to be on top," she'd said. He remembered his blubbering response. "What?"

"I need someone who will be in control," she'd said.

"Okay," he'd muttered, not knowing if he'd won the sex lottery or stepped into a trap with the vice squad. He promised himself not to agree to pay her for sex, a promise he wasn't sure he could keep.

Della clarified her intentions with the implied suggestion of a sexual reward to follow. It helped that her situation was intriguing, with accusations of murder in the air. She was excited that one or both of the other two authors who were going to be on the show intended to kill Raspy and Salty and she needed Mike's help. She reeled him in with her promise to share 25 percent of the profits from her soon-to-be released bestselling book about how she stopped the crime.

"Mikey, honey, you need to focus."

Mike shook his head. "Got it." He tried not to let his eyes wander to the cleavage revealed by her low-cut blouse.

"Tell me about your recent conversation with Salty Remarks."

"She wanted to know how we connected. I told her I had the hots for you and reached out, but you blew me off."

Della purred. "Sounds like Chapter 5 in my novella *Heartbreak at Rocky Knob*. Well done, Mikey. Did you tell her I was seeking information about them?"

"I did. Just like you asked. I could tell she was on edge."

Della threw her head back and squealed, pushing her chest in Mike's direction. "Perfect. It's all about tension, Mikey. Remember that. Tension in every space, at every moment, in every nook and cranny, right until—"

Mike's phone buzzed, and he glanced at the number. "Excuse me," he said, putting the phone to his ear. The voice he heard was one he'd heard before. It asked him to say "yes" or "no" in response to one question. "Is she committed?" It was an easy "yes," he said, and then he clicked off and turned his attention back to Della, who had moved closer to him on the love seat.

"I need to ask a favor, Mikey." She whispered in his ear that she needed something from him. "A diversion."

His head spun. "You want a diversion, now?" He glanced at

the office door, hoping his purple-headed high school employee wouldn't come asking for him.

"No, silly. I need it tonight. Heavy smoke at five minutes left in the podcast show. Enough black smoke to cover the stage and create a sense of panic in the room."

Mike felt disappointment but not for long. Della leaned in and kissed him, slow and long. "And one more teensy-weensy thing."

Mike gulped.

"I need you to smuggle in a slow-acting poison. A small vial will do. I wrote it down for you. The name and where to find it." With one hand, she pulled a rolled paper from her brassiere and tucked it in Mike's pocket. She placed her other hand on his thigh and rubbed back and forth. "Can you do that, Mikey?"

Mike thought back to her explanation that her goal was to stop a murder. Maybe that was true. Maybe it wasn't. If it wasn't and Raspy and Salty departed this earth tonight, he'd be fine with that. He'd dreamed of implementing his own Plan B —*Better off dead*—to be done with the *Under the Covers* sponsorship, but a solution by someone else's hand was better.

When Della leaned in for another kiss, Mike thought about the dangerous multi-sided game he had played and how he hadn't been honest with Della or Salty. The anonymous voice on the phone belonged to the person who wired him $5,000 to lure Salty and Raspy to the bookstore after the event without telling Della that William Wisp and Edwin Nocturne would be there. Mike suspected this was the fail-safe. If Della didn't get Salty and Raspy at the event, William and Edwin would get them at the bookstore. Either way, he was in the catbird seat.

Penny Leverage was about gaining the upper hand in anything she did. It bothered her to no end that Raspy and Salty had fallen behind in their payments and had cajoled her into providing the audio team and a security guard for their event tonight. They were going to be in debt to her even more. And that was why, when her benefactor transferred $5,000 into her account, she agreed to cooperate.

Penny's first assignment had been to contact struggling poet William Z. Wisp and pretend to be his audiobook savior. Little did she realize the call would lead to a better offer by the poet, a 25 percent share of the profits in his bestselling true crime book about two dead podcasters, plus the audio rights to the book.

The intercom on her desk buzzed. "A Mr. Wisp to see you, ma'am."

"Show him in."

Penny walked around to the front of her desk and welcomed the diminutive poet into her office. The seat she offered guests for meetings was a few inches lower than her own, which gave her a dominant view. She asked if he wanted a coffee or cola but he declined. He hugged his colorful tote bag to his chest when he sat. "Big night tonight," she said.

He was all business. "You've done what I asked?"

"I have. Misdirection all around. Anonymous text messages. And a tall tale about how you and I connected, although I'm sure Raspy Fuse doesn't believe my love of poetry brought us together, or that I have a love of poetry at all. No offense intended."

William Z. Wisp raised his eyebrows and the lines on his face tightened. "What about the bookstore reading?"

"He bought it," Penny said. "But he seemed surprised."

"That's good," William said. "If they believe two of the three authors are hanging around for a local reading after the event, they may feel safer and become less vigilant during the show itself. Whatever happens is going to happen during the event. The bookstore set-up is the back-up plan."

Penny hadn't trusted William Z. Wisp from the first day she met him, but what he said had a ring of truth to it. The drama would be better if things went down while the mics were live and the audience was present. Bigger splash. Better book. "I've told my security guard if things go south, he must grab Raspy and Salty—preferably by force—and rendezvous at the bookstore."

William reached into his bag and pulled out a small handgun. "I need you to slip this past the security team tonight and get it to me before the show starts."

Penny stared hard at William, and he looked away, down at his feet. He didn't have the killer vibe, but one never knew.

"I can't stop Della or Edwin without this," he said.

Penny didn't believe he was there to be a hero. He was too bitter at the world. And too pompous about poetry. He was liable to shoot all prose writers in the room, starting with Della and Edwin. Maybe that was his plan. Maybe he was going to shoot them and make it look like they were about to kill Salty and Raspy. "You can't stop poison with that gun."

"They won't use the same method twice. They're terrible writers, not idiots."

Penny looked at the gun on the front of her desk. William

could go to jail for whatever he had in mind. And he could take her with him. "Fifty percent," she said.

His already gigantic eyes grew wider. "That's half the profits on the book."

Penny pushed the gun back toward him with a pen. They didn't call her Penny Leverage for nothing.

When the poet was gone, she looked at the gun and thought about the future. She sent a text to Mike Reader that said,

> See you at the bookstore tonight after the show.

She took out her phone. She had one more call to make to her deadbeat ex-husband.

TAKE 9

FOUR AUTHORS IS A CROWD

Raspy watched familiar sights come into view as he drove Salty's Jeep across the North Carolina state line and back toward Charlotte: signs for Bojangles, towering pines, and First in Freedom flyers on the license plates. Their trip to New York had confirmed that one of the three authors on their panel tonight intended to kill them, but they'd agreed on the ride home that the doctor was not doing as much as she could to stop them. He glanced at Salty, who was more quiet than usual, less her sarcastic self.

Raspy grew up going to church every Sunday—no cuts allowed—a tradition he'd left behind when he went to college, and discontinued further when he came to Charlotte. Being from a large Southern family with a grandmother who made sure of his and his siblings' attendance, he'd never had a choice about whether to take in the word of God and never had the privilege to dip into the sanctuary for a few hymns, a Bible verse or two, and a quick sermon. For him and his family, church was more like a seventh-day-of-the-week marathon, but man he loved the afternoon lunches on the lawn with fixings from barbecue to Brunswick stew. The thought of the potluck made his mouth water. The thought of how he'd ignored God for years made him worry.

"You ever attend church as a kid?" Raspy asked.

Salty turned down the radio. "Not much. Just weddings and funerals my mom dragged us to. When dad died, she left the church. Figured God wasn't looking after us. I was eight."

"Were you baptized?"

"What's this about?" Salty asked.

Raspy thought about his grandmother. *You better get right with the Lord* was her constant refrain. He smiled thinking about Grandma. He could see her sitting in her pew on Sunday in her all-white dress waving that big fan in her face and whacking him with it when he and his friends talked while the minister did. She whispered—though everyone in the church could hear because they said "Amen" when she finished warning them— how they might never know when the Good Lord was going to call them home, and "he needs to have your number handy when he does, which he won't have if you two ain't on the list." Was he on the list? He wasn't sure.

"Oh, it's nothing," Raspy said, but he knew it wasn't nothing.

"You're not thinking about dying on me today, are you?" There it was, the Salty he knew and loved. "Pull over," she said. "I'll drive the rest of the way. We can plan as we drive."

With Salty at the wheel, they made a list and Raspy made the calls. He confirmed the venue, an old movie theater with a large stage and stadium seating. He talked with their media contacts. They had the event on their calendar. He reminded Barry

Bookum of the when and where for his clients. Barry wished them luck. He discussed the audio set-up with the leader of Penny Leverage's audio crew. They were ready.

Next, Raspy called Dan the IT Man to discuss the live video feed. Dan said he was "on it" and "not to worry," that he'd have everything ready for them, with an enthusiasm that seemed out of place for a guy who only wanted to get paid. The last call was to Mike Reader, who said promotion was going well, that they should have a big crowd. "And don't forget to come by the bookstore for beers after the event," he said. "I'm looking forward to putting things right with you and Salty." Like Dan the IT Man, Mike's voice was too pleasant for a guy who wanted nothing to do with them a few days ago.

For the next thirty minutes, they talked about how to run the show. An interview of several authors at one time is tricky business. Exuberant authors can dominate the time with long-winded self-serving answers, resulting in boring soliloquies, but the flip side is problematic too, where hesitant authors offer ten-second answers. They'd need to balance the questions among their guests while keeping the conversation interesting. They agreed they'd save the juiciest question for last, the one about who killed podcaster Stacy Story.

Salty pulled next to the curb in front of Raspy's NoDa home, a well-shaded Craftsman converted into duplex apartments, just as Raspy's phone rang. Salty killed the engine, and Raspy answered on speaker. "Penny, I've got Salty with me. What's up?"

"Everything is in place with the audio crew and my security guy. But there's been a change in plans with Rocky. He's not coming on the show tonight."

Raspy and Salty looked at one another before Raspy asked the question. "Any reason?"

"He must have heard about your ratings."

It felt like Penny smiled through the phone even though she was the one who'd pleaded to get her ex-husband on the show. Was Rocky no longer interested, or was something else at play here?

Raspy said goodbye to Penny, ended the call, and turned to Salty, whose frown mirrored the confusion he felt. "Call Rocky," Salty said. "Let's get his side of the story."

As the phone rang, Raspy put it on speaker and set it on the dashboard between them. Rocky answered on the fourth ring. "What's up?"

"Rocky, Salty here. We heard you're bailing on us tonight. What gives?"

"Nuttin' to do with bail." Rocky sounded like he was talking from inside a barrel, but then Raspy remembered from the one time he'd seen Rocky that he was the barrel. "Or parole, or prison, or murder plots, or any of that. I done my time and want no part of the crime what's going down tonight."

"What do you mean?" Raspy asked, knowing full well what Rocky meant.

"Don't want no PO-lease blaming me for your murder just 'cause I served time."

"Nobody's getting murdered," Raspy told him, hoping he sounded more assured than he felt now that Penny was involved in the plot and likely tipped Rocky off.

"Not what I heard."

Salty came to Raspy's rescue. "Hey Rock. We want to help you tell your story."

There was brief silence on Rocky's end. "Never wanted to do this with lots of people watching, but Penny pushed me. Said it would help with sales to pay her the back alimony I owe her. Until today, that's all she's cared about."

"What do you mean 'until today'?" Salty asked.

"She called me today and told me your number was up and I needed to steer clear."

Salty bent one leg over the other and leaned closer to the phone. "Rocky, suppose there were a way we could wipe your slate clean with Penny, and help you tell your story without the bright lights and people watching. Would that suit you?"

"What's the catch? There's always a catch."

Salty took her time. She told Rocky what they knew about the danger they faced tonight with the three authors and explained what they needed from him.

Rocky went silent again, for so long that Raspy wondered if he had ended the call. Then Rocky spoke from the bottom of his barrel. "I'll think about it." he said, and the call was over.

Salty looked at Raspy and shrugged. "At least we tried," she said.

Raspy stuck his phone in his pocket, grabbed his notes, and exited the vehicle. When he shut the door, he leaned through the open window and faced Salty. "We're down to three deranged authors, Salt, one of whom wants to kill us with help from Penny. Any last words?"

"Call Doctor Toomey like we discussed. This ends tonight. See you at the theater in one hour. And please, take a shower."

Raspy made the phone call and walked as he talked. The conversation didn't last long because it was the one-sided kind, with him doing most of the talking. After the defense they'd been playing, it felt good to try a little offense.

When Raspy was done with what he had to say—the message being Doctor Toomey had better tell her patients to back off or else the medical board would hear about her negligence—her response was so cryptic, he wrote it down. He and Salty hoped Toomey would alert the authors that Raspy and Salty were on to them, causing the culprit to make a mistake and tip his or her hand before it was too late.

Raspy put his key in his front door lock and turned. The motion opened an unsettling thought. What if William Z. Wisp, Della Molasses, Edwin Nocturne, and all their helpers were full grown grizzlies, not inexperienced cubs? It made him wonder if poking the bears was such a good idea after all.

When he closed the door behind him, something clicked in his brain about the comment Toomey had made to him: "You can't stop a bestseller that was meant to be."

TAKE 10

WHERE THERE'S SMOKE THERE'S MYSTERY

Raspy peeked between the drawn velvet stage curtains at the Carolina Theater, a beautiful historic venue in uptown Charlotte with an Art Deco façade. The large chattering crowd made his nerves spike. Did the killer have allies in the house, whose movements would be hidden when the lights went down? He squared his shoulders, steadied his breathing, and told himself to ignore that thought.

Salty tapped his shoulder. "Ready?"

He turned to face her. "Let's do this."

When the podcast theme music played, Raspy and Salty walked onstage to polite applause. They settled in chairs behind a table that faced the audience, adjusted their table mics, and gave each other a fist bump. Salty led off with a version of their trademark introduction: "Welcome to this live production of the *Under the Covers* podcast, where books and writing topics are center stage, and where authors give voice to their written words." More applause. Louder this time.

Raspy followed with introductions, doing his best to match Salty's enthusiasm. "You know our first guest as a master of mystery, suspense, and chills—he's a thriller writer with a wild imagination. His recent novel *Blood on Her Hands* is turning heads and pages. Please give it up for Edwin Nocturne!"

Edwin came out, dressed in a black suit and white shirt buttoned up to the neck, and nodded to the crowd's applause with a tight smile. He took a seat on the long sofa facing the audience, touched the lavalier mic on his lapel, and reached for a water glass on the coffee table. He took a sip before sitting back, erect.

Feeling the energy in the room, Raspy ad-libbed a bit. "Are there any poetry lovers in the house? Anyone who enjoys the tight imagery of a good stanza? If so—" he said to dying applause, "you're in for a real treat tonight. Please welcome our second guest, award-winning poet and lecturer William Z. Wisp!"

William entered wearing a flowing caftan with a bolo necktie. Raspy didn't understand the sartorial logic, or much of anything else about William or his poetry. Their poet took a seat at the other end of the sofa as far as he could get from Edwin.

Raspy looked across the stage where their third guest waited in the wing. She blew him a kiss on cue. "Does anyone love romance?" A woman hooted. "How about sex? Anyone care for that?" Male and female voices shouted their approval this time, followed by laughter, and the best applause yet.

"Okay then. Let's meet a woman who analyzes her prose from every position and whose tales are yoga-class flexible, with a balance of satisfyingly quick chapters and chapters that take at least sixty pleasant minutes to finish. Please welcome the lovely, sexy romance novelist, Della Molasses!"

Della sashayed onstage wearing—well, not much. Her V-cut blouse left as little to the imagination as her bedroom scenes. She leaned over the interview table and kissed Salty on the lips, and when Salty played along, Raspy had no choice but to do the same. Della bounded to the sofa and took her seat between the poet and the thriller writer, where she announced to the audience's pleasure that it had been a while since "I had a threesome in public." Raspy noticed Mike Reader grin from a front-row seat. He yielded to Salty to kick off the interviews.

"Let's begin with a few questions about each of your latest books, starting with you, William. Your collection's title poem, 'For My Mother on the Day She Becomes a Bird,' is an example of a pantoum, with an adapted quintet for the final stanza. Can you tell us about how the repetition in the poem expresses the cyclical nature of family trauma?"

Raspy smiled to himself at the level of Salty's preparation. They had discussed getting the authors comfortable and in good spirits early by asking friendly questions and praising their work, and Salty's researched approach seemed to work when William's wide, gleaming eyes lit up. "Of course. I love talking about the role of repetition, almost as much as I love talking about family trauma."

Next, they explored point of view choices for thrillers and romance books. Edwin liked the close third person POV for his thrillers so his readers could get inside the evil-doer's head—something Raspy thought would be helpful for him and Salty to do before the night was over—and Della liked the first person POV for the emotional feel it evoked for readers, "particularly," she said with a wink, "when feeling is an important part of the story."

They talked about author inspiration, about inciting incidents, about three-act structures, about poetic forms, and about satisfying endings, something Della found essential and William thought overblown, "since not everything needs to be spelled out," he said.

Raspy enjoyed the conversation despite the stress of the night. Giving authors a chance to tell their stories—and the stories behind their stories—was what he loved most about the podcast.

"Edwin," Salty asked, "what's one piece of advice you would give to your younger writing self?"

Edwin rubbed his chin. "Read widely and deeply, and start with an outline, especially for a complex plot like a thriller. And don't be afraid of the power of a shocking twist, like a surprise death."

"Of a character," William added, with a glance at Edwin.

"Yes, yes, of a character," Edwin said.

"Good advice," Salty said. "How about you, William?"

William took a deep breath and looked at the rafters. "I would not impart any advice to my younger self. I would let myself suffer the knocks and blows. Every tragedy has made me keenly attuned to life's rich symphony."

"An interesting viewpoint," Raspy said. "Della, what advice would you give to yourself as a younger writer?"

Della took her time as she uncrossed and recrossed her legs, à la Sharon Stone in *Basic Instinct*. "If it gets your blood pumping, you're on the right track."

Raspy was about to follow up when William jumped in. "It's dust," William said.

"Excuse me?"

"The piece of advice to my younger self. If I had to say, I'd say: You are dust, and to dust you will return."

"Like Stacy Story?" someone shouted.

The voice came from the back of the room. Raspy squinted into the dark house, but couldn't tell who had asked the question.

"Which one of you killed her?" someone closer to the front yelled.

The dark auditorium concealed the face of a stocky man in the same row. He leaned forward—his face still hidden—as if he were interested in who would cop to the crime. Nervous and excited chatter rippled through the audience. The authors shifted in their seats. Raspy looked at Salty, who gave him a small nod.

Raspy's heart pumped at a faster pace, but he kept his voice calm. "Edwin, do you know if someone murdered Stacy Story?"

Someone in the front row was impatient. "Just ask him if he did it."

William gathered his notes and rose, but Della pushed him back in his seat. "Not so easy, lover boy."

Raspy noticed that several people in the audience raised their phones, recording what the author of the bestseller *Blood on Her Hands* was about to say. "Just tell us what you remember about the night she died." He tried to calm Edwin, but he knew the can of worms was open and things could get messy soon.

Edwin sat with a stiff posture. "Nothing much to tell. During the interview, I talked about my newest release *A*

Scream in the Willows. Ms. Story's questions were surface-level, all things she could have gleaned from Goodreads. I don't think she had read the book. The interview ended. I went home and relaxed with a Bloody Mary. The next day, I heard the news."

Raspy knew enough about Stacy Story's death from the internet accounts to know that Edwin was lying. By the murmurs coming from the audience, they sensed it too.

The poet edged to the front of the sofa and touched his stack of chapbooks on the coffee table. "Must we wade these grisly waters? Wouldn't it be better to hear about the space between the poet and the first-person poetic self?"

Della answered for the audience. "That's a negatory, William. Literally no one wants to hear about that." She pulled a piece of paper from the pages of her romance book. "But they might be interested in a reading from your bank records, specifically the line item where you received $25,000 for conspiring with Edwin to murder Stacy Story."

William made a high-pitched noise of outrage. "That's slander."

Edwin paled at the accusation, but he mustered enough energy to chime his me-too. "I will sue you…you…you…harlot."

"Ha," Della said. She pulled more paper from her book. "I can also do a dramatic reading from your early draft for *Blood on Her Hands,* a book eerily similar to the story of Ms. Story's death, a draft which was completed a few days before she died!"

Now the audience was abuzz. White lights glowed from all the raised phones. "Let's keep this civil," Salty called, but their three guests were on edge.

Della gave a tiny nod to the audience and Raspy followed her gaze to where he saw Mike Reader pull out some kind of electronic device from between his legs and tap it. An acrid smell distracted Raspy. Like burning leaves. Then tendrils of black smoke crept out from under the stage. They soon grew into billowing clouds. People in the front rows coughed and choked, covering their faces with their hands and arms as they jumped from their seats.

"Everybody stay calm! Head for the exits!" Salty shouted.

Raspy stood, and as the smoke overwhelmed the stage, he saw Della pull a medical mask and rubber gloves from inside the neckline of her shirt. She donned the mask, then snapped the gloves on.

Within seconds, the three authors disappeared in the smoke. Bam.

Screams rang out at the sound of the gun.

Raspy's mic flew off the table to his left and hit the floor. He leaned over to pick it up and noticed a hole through the center. He lunged toward Salty and pulled her down—just as another shot fired and a knife sailed through the smoke where Salty had stood.

They caught each other's eyes but had no time for words. They army-crawled toward one wing of the stage. The stage floorboards rattled beneath them as feet flew by—the only body parts visible in the smoke—and in their effort to escape, shrieks surrounded them.

When they made it offstage where the smoke was thinner, Raspy sat up against an equipment crate, coughed, and rubbed his eyes. "Are you okay?" he asked Salty.

"I think so. You?"

"Yeah, but—" He stopped when Della hurried past them in her gold-spiked heels. She scampered towards William and

Edwin—both slumped on the floor nearby—where she bent and handed them each a glass of water.

"You need to drink, clear your throats," she encouraged in a loud voice. They gulped the water, dazed. She pulled a gun from William's hand—a gun? From William's hand? Had wormy little poet William Z. Wisp almost killed him with a gun?

Raspy cupped his ear to hear Della's next words. "You shouldn't be caught with this," she said to Edwin. She pointed a knife at him. "Nor should you have left this behind with your prints all over it." It must have been the blade that almost got Salty.

Why was Della Molasses helping William Z. Wisp and Edwin Nocturne? She hated them more than she hated missing out on a good time.

The black-clothed security guard Penny Leverage had hired pulled Raspy and Salty to their feet. "You two. With me. Now."

Raspy heard sirens and saw a firefighter step on the stage. He wondered if he should stay and help, but decided it would be smarter to leave it to experienced first responders and follow their protector to safety. When he looked back, he saw his author guests scatter. Edwin and William went one way together. Della went another. Seconds later, Rocky Fist appeared from behind a curtain and looked in one direction, then the other. He followed the path Della had taken.

TAKE 11

DEATH AT THE BOOKSTORE

As the itch of smoke cleared from her eyes and throat and her breathing settled, Salty had a question for Raspy, who sat next to her in the van's backseat. "Do you know where we're going?"

"Away from where we were, and that's good," Raspy said, massaging his temples.

Salty squinted at snatches of the passing neighborhood through the black windows. Dumpsters overflowed. Shadowed figures passed into and out of the radiuses of flickering streetlights. "Hey, where are you taking us?" Salty called up front. No response. "Excuse me, can you tell us where we're going?" Still no answer. She sat up straighter.

"Let us out," Raspy commanded, but again, no response.

They reached for their door handles and pulled. Locked. Seriously? They had escaped a smoke bomb, gunshots, and a flying knife, only to be abducted?

The van ground to a halt under the glowing green sign of Mike's Used Bookstore. Salty's door slid open, but before she could get an explanation from Penny's security guard as to why he had brought them here—a place they planned to come anyway before their world turned violent—the barrel of a gun greeted them. "Straight into the bookstore," their captor told them.

Mike Reader met them at the door. He didn't smell of smoke, as if he'd known how to avoid it. "Glad you could make it."

"Mike, what's this about?" Raspy asked, but Mike didn't answer. He locked the door and walked away. They followed with the gun-pointing guard on their heels.

Mike stopped in the children's area near the back of the store. "I thought this would be a good place for the reading. As our special guests, you will sit there."

The guard forced them with rough pushes to their shoulders to sit on primary-colored beanbags, with murals of Winnie the Pooh and Peter Rabbit behind them. Once in the chairs, it was hard to get up without rolling sideways and exerting effort. Not the best spot for a quick escape.

Beside them were three folding chairs. "Those chairs are for Penny, Dan, and me," Mike said. "We're all fans of our guests and wouldn't miss their reading for anything."

Penny Leverage and Dan the IT Man came in and took their seats without saying a word, and Salty sized up their predicament. To their backs was a solid wall with children's books and posters. To one side, Penny, Dan, and Mike flanked them. The guard leaned against the wall on the other side with his gun in hand. Six feet in front of them were two empty club chairs.

"Ah, here are our guests of honor," Mike said. He, Penny, and

Dan clapped for William Z. Wisp and Edwin Nocturne as they entered. Mike ushered the writers into the club chairs.

Salty remembered Mike's invitation a few days ago to her and Raspy to come to the bookstore after the show—it would be just the three of them to have a few cold beers and make a fresh start—and their confusion when Penny Leverage told Raspy that William Wisp and Edwin Nocturne would do a reading here instead. "Mike," she asked. "Why all the misdirection about this meeting? Is this your idea of a fresh start? Making us listen to poetry at gunpoint?"

"I misspoke, Salty. It's more like a fresh ending."

Mike's response irritated Raspy. "It was only a $3,500 sponsorship deal, Mike. Hardly worth holding us hostage."

Mike laughed. "There's more at play now. And don't worry. You won't be hostages much longer. Things are going to end for you soon." He turned to the poet and the thriller writer and said, "It's your show."

Salty glanced at the security guard, who waggled his gun in their direction. She turned her attention back to the two club chairs, where Edwin scribbled on a piece of paper and William fidgeted with his hands. When Edwin looked up, he spoke five words. "You should already be dead."

That seemed like a fair analysis to Salty, and she couldn't help herself. "You failed with the revolver and the knife. What are you going to try next? The lead pipe? The rope? The candlestick? The wrench? Or do you even have a clue?"

"I have a clue," Edwin said. "I'm touching up the ending as we speak. Just a slight tweak to the plot since you're still breathing." He didn't elaborate.

They needed to do something. But what? Salty took several

anxious breaths as she looked at the rows of books on the shelves. Millions and millions of words surrounded them, but as she thought about that, her breathing relaxed. This was her and Raspy's natural habitat. Words were their thing. In fact, words were the only weapon they had left. It was time to use them. Time to parley.

She directed her gaze at William Z. Wisp. "Isn't this the part of the story when the would-be killer explains their motivation to kill the soon-to-be-deceased victim and describes the grotesque ending they have in mind for them? Oh, but you wouldn't know about that. You're just a poet."

William took the bait. "Everyone says poets can't plan a story. That we only know how to wax lyrical when we feel inspired. Not me." His cheeks had turned pink, and a scrim of sweat gleamed on his face.

"Everyone wants blood and guts," he continued. "They want truth, not content with imagination. I will capitalize on that with actual murders—your murders—to create a bestseller, the way Edwin did with Stacy Story's death. But my scheme is better, because thanks to Penny Leverage, there will be an audiobook, and thanks to Dan—who knows how to run a podcast—there will be a podcast too. I'll make enough money to do whatever I want. Self-publish my poetry, start my small press, or just live off the royalties and not have to suffer through a day job in that place where poetic dreams go to die: academia. I am buying creative freedom. And the best part is— thanks to your role in this drama—it will be true crime, not the formulaic schlock thriller writers churn out again and again." He turned to Edwin. "No offense," he said.

"None taken," Edwin said, as he continued to scribble.

Salty tried the pry and divide approach. "Why team up with Edwin Nocturne? He's more successful than you. Better writer too."

William blanched. Sweat beaded his forehead. "You…you—"

Edwin reached over and placed his hand on William's arm to calm him. "Don't let them get to you. Everything is under control."

Edwin's color was high too, and he squirmed before he addressed Salty and Raspy. "When William approached me, his offer was too good to turn down. He said he would commit the crime, which set me at ease—I'm an expert at writing murders, but didn't relish the idea of enacting one. For a poet, William's pretty ruthless. Not very good with his aim, though. He was supposed to shoot you both. Missed each time. My knife was a distraction."

William shrugged and tugged at his collar.

"Why all the subterfuge about a bookstore reading?" Raspy asked Edwin.

"Oh, there will be a reading," Edwin continued. "William thought it would be poetic that you hear us read the death scene before it happens. Great drama for the story."

"You're forgetting one thing," Salty said. "You're implicating yourselves."

Edwin coughed and patted his chest. He nodded to William to explain, but William seemed in distress too. Penny Leverage did the honors. "You've seen the credits, Salty. The ones that say 'This movie is based on a true story.' Which means somebody ripped the truth apart and made it more interesting. I can't wait to read the final draft, the way William and Edwin pin your deaths on that freak, Della Molasses."

Raspy addressed Penny. "Was this reading your idea?"

Penny smiled. "Group effort. It was the back-up plan, but one I hoped would have to be put into play. It adds to the twists and turns, don't you think?"

"One more question," Salty said to everyone in the room. "We know the roles of everyone here but one. William is supposed to commit the murders. Edwin is supposed to write about them. Penny is supposed to produce the audiobooks. And Dan is supposed to run the podcast. I don't see a role for Mike."

Before anyone could answer, glass shattered, a door opened, and footsteps approached. After a few seconds, Della Molasses, in all her sexed-up glory, stood before them, a small caliber gun in one gloved hand, a throwing knife in the other.

"Honey, I'm home," she said to Mike. Then she shot the security guard in the head with William Z. Wisp's gun.

Salty flinched. And except for the sound of the guard hitting the floor, the room went silent.

Mike ignored the dead guard slumped on the floor beside Raspy, walked to Della, and gave her a tight hug. His face melted into a grin. "I knew you'd make it."

"Sure you did. That's why I had to find out about this meeting on my own and why you locked the door. Don't you think I know you're cheating on me? Wire transfers. Secret calls with my therapist to track my movements. Come on, now. You've been a naughty boy, Mikey. You picked the wrong team to play for. Now take your seat with the other losers." She waved both weapons to direct Mike, whose shoulders sagged, to the empty chair between Dan and Penny.

Della then addressed the beanbag hostages. "How's it hanging, Raspy?" And to Salty, she said, "You are a good kisser. Shame really, for the both of you."

At first, Salty had thought Della might be their savior, come to bust up the party, prevent their murders, and soak up the publicity for her heroic deed. But no. Everybody in this room wanted to be a true crime writer. "Not you too," Salty said.

"Oh, don't be so shocked. I warned you. How did I put it in my text: 'Not to be dramatic—more like deadly accurate—one of the three author guests you and Salty plan to interview Tuesday night intends to kill you both.' You had three days to figure it out, and you failed. Miserably, I might add."

"How about a reading?" Raspy asked Della.

"What?"

"William and Edwin were about to entertain us with the edited version of the story of how we die and how they're going to profit off our murders. Care to give us the same favor?"

"William and Edwin are going to profit, are they?" Della pointed Edwin's knife and William's gun in their direction. Both men were paler, almost green. "This is Barbie's time," Della chirped. "Down with the patriarchy and all that jazz."

Salty expected Edwin and William to protest, jump up, do something—but they slumped farther into their chairs. William clutched his stomach, Edwin his chest. She could hear their tortured breathing from across the room.

"Oops, sorry about that," Della told the panting authors, shaking her head. "That looks unpleasant."

"Is this—" Edwin gasped.

"Arsenic," Della finished. "I got the idea from Chapter 19 of your thriller, *Out of the Shadows*."

"You monster!" Edwin choked.

"Is that any way to talk to a devoted reader?"

Della turned toward Raspy and Salty. "You want the story? Fine. Let's start with the slow-acting poison that's now doing its job on a whiny poet and pompous prose writer. I put the poison in the water they drank after they inhaled too much smoke. It appears they were quite thirsty."

Edwin gurgled and his body convulsed.

Della leaned in close to Edwin and whispered in his ear, loud enough for everyone to hear. "You were too greedy, Edwin. You manipulated me to kill Stacy Story—and it was work; she held her poison much better than you gentlemen appear to be doing—and you stole my story without sharing the profits."

Salty was curious. "You're killing Edwin for revenge?"

Della giggled. "That, plus I'm weeding out the competition. The public deserves a story much better than the mess Edwin and William tried to cobble together. Mine will be a romantic true crime story. It will be about five people with a profit motive and a hired security guard who all want you dead and a romance author heroine who figures the whole thing out after a bookstore owner seduced and betrayed her—it's true, I slept with Mikey to get him to help me and add a little sizzle to the story, but the sizzle was fizzle. I'll have to improve on his bedroom performance in the book." Mike made an indignant noise.

"Anyway, this heroic romance author—" Della did a curtsey, "solves the mystery but alas, the climax of her investigation and the climax of your deaths don't match up. You die first. She comes on the scene slightly later than necessary to save your lives. It happens sometimes."

"Why kill William?" Raspy asked.

Della laughed. "Besides the fact the publishing world won't miss having one less poet? He threw in with Edwin and cut me out. That's why. And he play-acted in front of our therapist that he was no murderer. The motive is revenge against him too, but for crossing me *and* for hypocrisy."

Salty tried not to look at the dead body on the floor as she vied for more time. "How did you stage this whole thing?" she asked Della.

"I paid Barry Bookum to book us together on another podcast. I didn't care whose. You can thank Barry for calling your number." She pointed to Edwin. "I was sure he would try to write another book about a dead podcaster. I figured he would convince William to kill you the way he convinced me to kill Stacy Story. Once things were in motion, I followed their greedy trail. And here we are."

"What about Dan, Mike, and Penny?" Raspy asked. "Where do they fit it?"

Della walked over to stand behind Dan, Mike, and Penny, where she had better control of the room and a better view of her gasping poison victims. She tapped Dan, Mike, and Penny on their backs with William's gun before she answered Raspy's question.

"When I learned Dan and Penny were helping Edwin and William, I hired Mike to help me. I then dug a little deeper to discover that Doctor Speak Toomey, our therapist, had her tentacles into Dan, Mike, and Penny, and they were feeding her information. My best guess is she thought she could stop the three authors from killing you.

"Oh—wait—" Della said. "I think William has something to

share." She held up a finger, and all eyes turned toward William, whose face was sallow and green-veined, his eyes closed. Everyone leaned in and strained to hear him.

"My soul escapes me with a sigh, and now at last at peace I…" His voice trailed off as he collapsed forward on the floor at Raspy's feet.

"Tsk tsk. So sad when a man doesn't finish," Della said. "Edwin? Are you about to die too?" Edwin gurgled. "Take your time," Della said. Edwin's breath grew harsher, like the sound of metal being filed—and then it stopped. Without a word, he fell forward on top of William. Salty flinched, the pellets in the beanbag chair crunching beneath her.

Della circled behind Raspy and Salty, stepped over the dead security guard, and leaned down to check William's pulse to be sure he was, in fact, a dead poet. She did the same with Edwin. When she appeared satisfied, she sat in Edwin's club chair, set the knife on one arm of the chair, and pulled out a folded sheaf of papers from within her shirt.

Della turned the gun on Dan, Penny, and Mike. "I'm afraid we've got some paperwork to do before you can go home." She tossed them each a pen. "It's time to sign your confessions to the murders of Edwin Nocturne and William Wisp."

"Confessions?" Dan the IT Man frowned as he read his paper.

"Yes." Della smiled. "Each of you conspired with William and Edwin on their murder-for-book-profit scheme and witnessed their gruesome work tonight. First, their killing of Raspy Fuse, by—sorry to give spoilers—a single gunshot wound to the chest, and then, their killing of Salty Remarks, by the single thrust of a blade to her throat." She looked at Raspy and Salty.

"Price of fame and glory, I'm afraid." Salty resisted the urge to protect her throat with her hand.

"And then," Della continued, "and this is the reason you killed William and Edwin: after you witnessed the murders, they cut you out of the money and, alas, you poisoned them—a crime of greedy passion, perhaps. You then hid the poison in the store—I've hidden it for you where you won't find it but the police will when they receive an anonymous tip."

"It won't work," Mike said. "Even if we sign these—"

Della pointed the gun at Mike. "You will sign."

"See, that's the problem," Mike said. "I can't poison William if you—pretending to be William—shoot me. Your story falls apart."

Della banged her forehead with the knife's hilt. "Got me there, Mikey. How about this? After I shoot you with William's gun, Penny and Dan will poison him for doing it." She aimed the gun at Mike. "Which version of the story do you prefer?"

Mike didn't answer but Penny did. "I don't care if you shoot Mike, but how do you explain the dead security guard?"

Della touched her chin with the barrel of the gun. "Let's see. Okay. How about this? The security guard tried to take the gun from William, the gun went off and killed him, and you wrestled the gun away from William and held him prisoner until the poison did its work. Sound good?"

Penny fell back in her chair. She scratched her signature on her confession and handed it back to Della. Dan and Mike did the same with theirs.

Della shook her auburn head, then swung the gun toward Raspy. "Your turn, Mr. Fuse. You should be grateful you're getting a bullet from William Z. Wisp and not the poison or the knife."

Salty's brain scrambled. She had to come up with words to dissuade or distract Della, or some clever way for them to escape. All the endings she'd read in books, where heroes thwarted villains, flooded back to her, but none seemed plausible in real life, when faced with a very real gun. Raspy looked just as lost.

Bam.

Della fired straight at Raspy's heart.

"Raspy!" Salty screamed.

He fell toward his left and crumpled, where his face folded into the beanbag. This couldn't be real. She placed both hands on his back and pleaded for him to get up, but Raspy didn't move. And for what? A stupid true crime story come to life?

Salty cried, but her tears soon gave way to anger. Nobody shot her best friend and got away with it. She had had enough of Della Molasses.

"Get up," Della encouraged. "I know how you think, Salty. It's why the story is playing out in this order."

Salty rolled herself out of the beanbag and stood with her hands clenched by her side. Della stood four feet away from her, gun down by her side in one hand, and knife outstretched in the other.

Della purred. "This is the part where you charge, Salty, and where Edwin Nocturne drives this knife into your throat."

"Drop your weapons or I shoot." The voice came from somewhere in the store's Mystery section.

When the man's figure emerged from the shadows, Salty tried to place him. She'd never met him but was sure she'd seen his author headshot, except the photo hadn't shown that nature and nurture had turned him into a Rottweiler. When he pointed his gun at Della and repeated, "Drop your weapons," she knew the man was Rocky Fist, the ex-con turned memoir writer and Penny Leverage's ex-husband.

Della backed away from Salty, let her knife hand fall to her side, and turned toward the voice. "Drop my weapons? And why should I do that? Are you going to give me something more dangerous to hold?"

"Geez Louise, woman, do you ever quit with the entendre?" Penny said.

"This is a romance story, darling. We play hard until the very end."

Rocky Fist walked closer to everyone and positioned himself where he was one corner of an imaginary square. The corner of the square across from him was where Salty stood beside Raspy's body. The corner to his left was where Mike, Dan, and Penny were on their feet in front of their chairs. And the corner to his right was where Della Molasses stood, with her arms by her side, a knife in her left hand and a gun in her right.

"I said drop your weapons, not just the arms holding them." Rocky's voice convinced Salty but Della didn't comply. Instead, Della was now the one vying for time.

"What's your part in this, Rocky Fist? When you tailed me from the theater, you cost me valuable time sending you on a wild chase in the wrong direction."

"That Uber switcheroo you pulled on me was pretty slick, but I realized my mistake halfway across town," Rocky said.

"Figured out where to find you, though, since Penny didn't want me here."

"Why are you here, Rocky?" Penny asked. "I forgave your debt to stay out of the way."

Rocky gesticulated freely with the gun. He swung it from Della to Penny and back toward Della. "I'm tired of taking your orders. In ten years of marriage, you never listened to ten words I said. But you and I aren't married anymore and I couldn't care less about the debt." He looked at Salty. "Someone made me a promise if I helped them tonight. I'm sticking with the people who want to give voice to my stories, not silence them."

"You came too late," Salty said. She tried to keep tears from her eyes as she looked down at Raspy's body.

"Sorry, Salty, I tried. Is Raspy—"

"Yeah, he's dead," Della said. "I am a better writer and a better shot than William Z. Wisp."

While Rocky aimed his gun at Della and Della gripped hers at her side, Salty knelt down and gently rolled Raspy over to look at his chest. No blood. That was a good sign, right? Then his lips moved—something between a sigh and a groan.

"Raspy!" she cried. "Come on, come on, you're okay." Then she noticed something odd. "Uh, Raspy? I know I've joked about you having a short fuse, but you're literally smoking." Black wisps of smoke poured out of his chest. Was spontaneous human combustion a thing?

Raspy dragged a hand up to his chest and winced as he felt around, then reached inside his shirt. He pulled out a handheld recorder that had a smoking bullet cratered into the center.

His voice croaked, but he sounded like his old podcast-worried self. "I don't think our audio is going to be very clear."

Salty grinned as she patted her chest and whispered so only Raspy and Della could hear. "That's why we always have a backup."

Just when Salty's heartbeat had returned to normal, a swift motion to her side caught her eye. Della, still covered by Rocky, had raised her gun hand back up and aimed it at Salty. Her face was fierce and twisted. "You're recording too? Think you're going to get your own book deal out of this? Maybe your own podcast? Screw you," she declared. "I may die, but I can still get the fame. Your recording will make the story that much better. People love a villain they can love to hate. I'm not letting a chance slip away from me again. This time, I'm coming first."

"Don't do it, Della." Rocky had both hands on his weapon, his feet spread. He wouldn't miss Della, but Della wouldn't miss Salty.

Salty watched Della as her grip on William Z. Wisp's gun grew tighter and her expression became more cartoonishly sinister. Above and behind Della on the wall was a poster that said it all. It was the cover of Salty's favorite children's book: *Where the Wild Things Are*.

One second later, the room filled with the sound of gunfire.

TAKE 12

THE SHOW MUST GO ON

Raspy rode in the ambulance when it transported Salty to the hospital from Mike's Used Bookstore—he insisted—and he waited outside the operating and critical care recovery rooms throughout a sleepless night. When the nurses moved Salty to her own room twenty-four hours later, he followed, still without sleep or anything to eat. He was ready to stay the night again until the attending doctor reported that Salty was sedated for the evening and urged him to go home, eat, and rest. He relented, but he didn't think he could sleep. There was work to do. He didn't yet know the complete story.

He arrived at his apartment and turned the key in the lock, and Sherlock scratched his paws against the other side of the door. The dog-friendly welcome by his bulldog was immediate and much-needed. Raspy knelt down to the floor, ran his hands along Sherlock's broad back, and nuzzled his face with his dog's. They then raced to the kitchen where Sherlock slid to a stop beside an empty food bowl. "Sorry buddy. I know you're hungry too."

"Akkk. Hungry too. Hungry too."

Raspy looked over his shoulder, and said to his parakeet, "Typo's next."

The parrot flapped his wings with apparent joy. "Typo next. Typo next. Akkk."

Once he'd fed his pets, he poured himself a bowl of Wheaties, gobbled it down, and then retraced his steps to the front door, where he picked up the canvas bag he'd laid on the floor. It was a tote for hauling books that read "Mike's Used Bookstore" on both sides. The night before, he'd seen it lying in the children's area and snatched it up to protect the evidence before the paramedics and police arrived. He retreated to his bedroom, where he pulled out Salty's digital recorder from the bag and set it on his bed.

The events of the previous evening were a blur after they fired the shots. Perhaps it was the adrenaline, or the fear of Salty dying, but for whatever reason, Raspy was having a hard time with the details. He remembered that just before Della fired her gun, he'd pushed Salty, hoping she'd fall out of harm's way. Though Della didn't miss and Salty was still in critical condition, the emergency room doctor said Raspy's push may have saved Salty's life. He also remembered applying pressure to her wound, something he'd read about characters doing in books.

Raspy had a vague notion—his grandmother got notions sometimes and told him never to ignore his—that he'd heard something important after Della shot Salty that confirmed why so many people wanted to kill him and Salty, but he couldn't recall what it was. He eyed Salty's recorder, wondering if it captured any intelligible words amongst the chaos. He turned it on and found the section of audio he wanted. Sherlock sat in the doorway and tilted his head at the sound of Della's voice.

"….People love a villain they can love to hate. I'm not letting a chance slip away from me again. This time, I'm coming first."

"Don't do it, Della."

Rocky had warned her, but it hadn't worked. The sound of gunfire was almost as loud as it had been in real time.

Screams and unintelligible voices filled the recording. Raspy heard his own voice. "Stay with me, Salty. Come on now, Salt, stay with me."

He heard a shuffling sound. This must have been when Raspy removed the recorder from beneath Salty's shirt and placed it in the bag, which he concealed under Salty's head, making it look like a pillow.

When he heard his own voice whisper a message, he remembered what he'd done next. To be sure, he took out his phone and checked his outgoing calls. Yep. He had called 911. Good thing. Because nobody else was interested in having medics or police anywhere near the place.

He heard Penny's voice next. "Is Della alive?"

"Not a chance," Rocky said. "I shot her in the chest."

"Then why is she moving?" Dan asked.

"Maybe," Della said, "it's because I am very much alive."

Della's miraculous survival wasn't what Raspy was listening for. He and Sherlock continued to pay attention to the audio.

The sound of a scrum followed, along with shouts and curses. An object hit the floor hard, followed by more objects. Books? Did someone knock over a bookcase?

"I've got her," someone said. "Give me some rope."

It sounded like Della struggled against the group's effort to secure her and screamed before someone muzzled her. "That tape should keep her quiet," Dan said.

For the next few minutes, Penny Leverage guided the conversation. Raspy turned up the volume on the recorder.

"Rocky," Penny said, "You need to leave. Possession of a weapon—a weapon permitted in my name that you took from my safe—violates your parole. Do you want to go back to prison?"

"How do I know you won't kill Raspy and Salty?"

"That's no longer your concern."

Raspy heard distant sirens, followed by a frantic word from Dan. "We've got to hurry."

"Now or never," Penny said to Rocky. "What will it be?"

"I'm taking the bullets from both them guns."

Good for Rocky. He hadn't been able to prevent the shootings, but he didn't leave until he had to and not before making it hard on the others to do more harm.

Footsteps receded as the sirens grew closer.

"He's gone," Mike said. "What now?"

"Get the confessions from Della," Penny said. "And destroy them. Hurry!"

The sound of grunts persisted until Mike said, "Got 'em. Who's got a lighter?"

Raspy recalled a trash can on fire and heard Dan's voice. "What's our story, Penny?"

"Call her," Mike said.

The notion that had been nagging at Raspy crystalized. It was the memory of a phone call to someone he and Salty suspected was the ringleader, the mama bear, and the puppet master all wrapped up in one.

"Calling now," Penny said.

Raspy could hear Salty's labored breathing and the sound of a voice on speaker.

"Hello, you've reached the voicemail of Doctor Speak Toomey with Author Rewrite Therapy Services. I can't take your call right now, but please leave a message. Your writerly health is important to me."

Penny's words tumbled out as soon as the beep sounded. "William and Edwin are dead. Just as you predicted. But we have a problem. Call as soon as possible."

A brief pause, then Penny said, "Let's get our stories straight. Come on! To the back."

For the next few minutes, Raspy heard himself offer encouragement to Salty to hang in there, telling her several times, "Help is on the way." It brought back the twist of anxiety he had felt in his stomach last night, especially since Salty's recovery was still uncertain.

He stopped the recorder and planned his next move. The wheels of justice might turn slowly for most people, but Raspy was true to his last name. He had a short fuse for criminals who tried to murder him and his best friend. It was time to light it.

TAKE 13
WHAT A DIFFERENCE A WEEK MAKES

Salty was now used to waking up in her hospital room with Raspy there. This time, she found him snoring in the recliner against the window with the drawn shades. He looked like his clothes hadn't been washed in days nor beard trimmed in a week, and his loyalty touched her. Ever since she awoke from her surgery—what was that, three, four days ago?—he had always been here for her.

With a spike of pain in her abdomen, she eased herself up in the bed and used the remote to raise her back and head. The whine of the bed's movement didn't shake Raspy from his slumber. Despite her pain, Salty was making the most of hospital life. Television, room service, a full-bed recliner. Not shabby.

The television played the noon news on mute. The headline at the bottom of the screen read "Investigation Continues into Double Homicide in Local Bookstore." Salty turned up the sound.

The reporter stood in front of Mike's Used Bookstore. She held a microphone and appeared very concerned, even with her fluorescent, on-camera makeup. "Your friendly neighborhood bookstore is supposed to be a center of learning and community. But at Mike's Used Bookstore in Charlotte, friendly… turned deadly. One week ago today, poet William Z. Wisp and thriller writer Edwin Nocturne died of arsenic poisoning inside the walls of this store." She pointed at the sign above the door and then turned back to the camera. "Today, author Della Molasses—known for her steamy romance books—was charged in the double homicide." A photo of Della, preening in pink lipstick, appeared in the upper right corner of the screen.

"Channel 24 has learned Ms. Molasses is likely to face other charges for the mayhem that occurred at the bookstore that night. Our sources tell us that the accused has hinted that she had accomplices, but is holding out for a reduced sentence plea deal for her cooperation. So far, there is no sign of a motive for the crimes. Stay tuned to Channel 24 for updates on this tale of books… and bloodshed."

Salty hit the mute button on the remote.

"I bet Mike doesn't care much for that publicity," Raspy said. "No parent is going to want to take their child to the reading circle of death."

Salty laughed. "Hello there, Sleeping Beauty."

Raspy stretched. "How ya doing, Salt?"

"Better and better, thanks to you and the excellent doctors and nurses."

Raspy stood and came to her bedside. She grabbed and held his hand. "You don't have to be here every day. Sherlock and Typo will miss you."

Raspy shrugged.

"But while you're here," Salty said, "bring me up to date."

The last report Raspy had given Salty was about his follow-up interview with the Charlotte detectives. They'd first interviewed him about Della, but after he shared with them the audio of what occurred in the bookstore, they came back to have him fill in some details.

"One detective called this morning," Raspy said. "The DA intends to charge Mike, Dan, and Penny with conspiracy to murder you and me."

Salty sighed. "I guess we'll have to testify."

"Unless they do a plea deal."

Salty shifted to get more comfortable. "What do they have to offer?"

"Come on Salt, the drugs haven't dulled your brain that much."

"They're going to give them Doctor Toomey?" Salty asked.

Raspy smiled. "I spoke with a New York detective last night who's been in touch with the Charlotte detectives. Penny has been singing the name of the good doctor and the other two canaries won't be far behind. The New York authorities are very interested in the case."

"And what do Penny, Dan, and Mike know?" Salty asked.

Raspy sat on the foot of the bed. "They know the doctor got them involved, paid them, promised them riches, and prodded them to be sure that either Della, William, Edwin, or any combination thereof, killed us."

"Is Della talking?" Salty asked.

"Not yet. But get this. Della has asked for an exclusive meeting with us, tape recorder included, against her lawyer's advice. The DA is fine with it as long as she pleads guilty, which she's agreed to do if we interview her. Apparently, fame is important to Della Molasses. Oh, and our three stooges—Mike, Penny, and Dan—want some guilty-plea airtime too, in the hope it will shave some time off their sentences."

Salty felt a surge of energy. "Speaking of getting back to recording… have you picked a name yet?"

"How about this: *The Making of a Podcast Murder*."

"I like it," Salty said. "Is the streaming company really going to pay us $150,000 to produce the podcast?"

"Yep, and that's just eight episodes. The company loves the fact that we have the real-time audio. And when we tell them about our exclusive interviews with the would-be-killers who were in the room when the shots were fired, the price could go up. If they like what we do, we may become true crime podcasters for good. And then there's the book deal to consider."

"So you're telling me I better hurry and get out of the hospital."

"Just doing my part to motivate you." Raspy's phone buzzed, and he answered.

Salty watched Raspy as he listened to the caller. During the five-minute call that seemed to go on forever, his face turned from serious to the biggest smile she'd seen on him in a long time. When he ended the call, the suspense of not knowing hurt Salty worse than her wound.

"That was the detective in New York. Based on affidavits from Penny, Mike, and Dan, they served a search warrant on Doctor Toomey this morning. You won our bet."

"Which one? The one about who was helping who, or the

one we made when we figured out what Doctor Toomey meant when she told you, 'You can't stop a bestseller that was meant to be'?"

"The second one, where you had a hunch about Doctor Toomey's writing style."

"That if her motive was to satisfy her writing dream by publishing a true crime story, she'd prepare an outline?"

"You got it. I was sure she'd write the story by the seat of her pants." Raspy reached in his pocket and pulled out a ten-dollar bill and dropped it in Salty's lap.

"They found an outline?" Salty asked.

"Yep, but not just a few beats for each chapter. It's very detailed. Names. Dates. Backstory—how she set everything in motion. I didn't get all the specifics, but after Stacy Story's death, Doctor Toomey solicited the three authors as clients through targeted referrals, and used their individual therapy sessions to get inside their heads as only a therapist can. She asked just the right questions to make them think killing you and me was their idea and that all she wanted to do was stop them."

"Clever," Salty acknowledged.

"The detective said her outline is as inside baseball as it gets. She had Mike, Dan, and Penny on retainer to feed her information and help the authors go through with the murders. It's quite Machiavellian."

"So that's it," Salty said. "The motive for everyone was the same? They wanted to profit off of our deaths with money from a true crime story?"

"Partly," Raspy said. "They all wanted us dead, but they wanted someone else to go down as the killer. Nobody expected to be the one charged with the crime, Doctor Toomey least of all, because she kept her physical distance and the physical blood from her hands."

Salty took a moment to process the state of things. "We have six people—seven if you count the dead security guard—who thought it would be profitable to kill us and write about it. They say crime doesn't pay. I suppose true crime doesn't pay, either."

"There's one exception," Raspy said. "True crime does pay for victims who keep their audio recorders running while the bad guys shoot at them."

Salty laughed. "Fair enough, Raspy. Call the nurse. My vacation is over. Time for us to get to work."

EPILOGUE

A FISTFUL OF MEMOIR

Raspy: Welcome, listeners, to episode 501 of the *Under the Covers* podcast. We have big news to share about an exciting new project, but more about that later. I'm here with my co-host Salty Remarks. Salty, great to have you on the mend and back in the podcast seat.

Salty: It's been a minute, Raspy, and I'm happy to be here. I'm excited about today's episode, because not only is our guest a writer whose book is uniquely him, he's the guy who broke up a podcast murder ring with a gunshot that saved my life.

Raspy: You're dead right, Salty. Our interview today is with Rocky Fist. He's a friend of the show, and a friend of ours. He served his time, wrote about it, and then served up justice to some criminal-minded opportunists. Rocky is the author of *My Life Behind Bars*, a collection of personal stories that take a behind-the-scenes look at the criminal justice system. Rocky, welcome.

Rocky: Glad to be here. When I watched you guys interview those authors at the theater, I knew I could trust you to help me tell my stories. Do y'all like my tortoiseshell glasses? The saleswoman said they make me look authorly.

Salty: I love them, Rock. Hey, before we talk about the shots fired in the bookstore, tell us what inspired *My Life Behind Bars*.

Rocky: If I'm being honest, Salty—something I'm trying to be from time to time now—my inspiration was boredom. Not much to do in prison.

Raspy: Can you share some titles of your personal stories?

Rocky: Sure. There's "My Little Bar of Soap." Oh, and "My Fight at Fried Chicken Night." And I wrote two stories about my roommate who passed away in his sleep. One is called "Don't Snore No More," and another is called "A Pinched Nose Blows No Air." Things like that.

Salty: Sounds interesting, Rock. Do you have a favorite?

Rocky: I'd have to say it's "Blow This Pop Stand in an Uber." It's about getting out of that dump of a prison.

Raspy: Never would have guessed that, Rocky. Thanks for clarifying.

Salty: Hey Rock, speaking of clarifying, our listeners would like to hear your take on what happened the night Della Molasses shot me, but first, Raspy has a word about that.

Raspy: Thanks Salty. Listeners, we're thrilled to share that in a few weeks, we will launch *The Making of a Podcast Murder*: a true crime podcast that delves into the efforts of seven people to kill yours truly and Salty too. You'll hear live audio interviews with the criminals, get a day-by-day breakdown of the events, learn about the motives behind the madness, and you'll hear audio from the night Rocky saved the day. This interview is just a prelude of what's coming.

Salty: We should add that Rocky told the truth to the authorities at the risk of going back to prison for violating his parole, but his information was so helpful to the police, they cut him a break. To be clear, he wasn't a snitch.

Rocky: Dead right, Salty. I'm no snitch. Just a guy who prevented a crime so he could sell some books.

Raspy: Tell us in your own words what you remember about that night, Rocky.

Rocky: I shot Della. She shot Salty.

Salty: Well put, Rocky. Listeners, you heard it here, straight from the man who saved my life. But Rocky's being modest. He shot several times. One shot went straight into the Winnie the Pooh mural. The other bullet went right for Della's heart—but a pocket mirror she had stuffed in her bra stopped it. Still not sure why the pocket mirror wasn't in an actual, you know, pocket, but hey, in this case, it saved her life. Now she lives to tell her lurid version of this tale.

Rocky: Della is a snitch.

Raspy: She is that Rocky, and a good thing for anybody who listens to *The Making of a Podcast Murder*, because they'll hear her confession and her indictments in her own words.

Salty: True that, Raspy. And we have a slight teaser here. Our listeners will also learn how a doctor in New York set the stage for the attempted murders through reverse psychology in order to fulfill her flickering dream of being a successful author. We will slice and dice the details, nuances, and emotional consequences of her actions in the upcoming podcast. That being said, the race is now on to see whether Della Molasses or Doctor Speak Toomey is the first to write and publish their true crime book from prison.

Rocky: Guys, that's gonna take a long, long time. They don't give you much paper in prison. And the pencils are stubby and dull. Cuts down on stabbings.

Raspy: That's what we're counting on, Rocky. Our true crime podcast and book will be out long before the criminals can scratch out their first drafts.

Salty: Speaking of prison, I hear Dan the IT Man is teaching a WordPress class to inmates, Mike Reader is driving the library book cart in his cell block, and Penny Leverage is running some kind of pyramid scheme in the clink.

Raspy: Got to hand it to them, they are resourceful. And with that prison primer, our time is up for today. We hope you enjoyed our interview with a unique author, a man who knows his way around a shoot-out. You'll hear more from him in *The Making of a Podcast Murder.*

Rocky: Happy for you both. You turned attempted murder into something positive. Couldn't have happened to two nicer folks.

Salty: Thanks, Rock, means a lot from a skilled attempted murderer like you.

Raspy: Speaking of attempted murder, if there's one thing I've learned from this entire experience, it's that everyone and his second cousin wants to turn killings into true crime bestsellers. So tell us Rocky, is that what you have in mind for your next book?

Rocky: Oh no! I've followed my true passion: middle grade fantasy. My story starts with a nine-year-old boy named Stony Fist. Stony is a big fella for his age, so everyone expects him to be a bully, and wants him to wrestle during recess. But all Stony really wants is a friend. And one day, he finds one when a magical pony gallops up to his bedroom window…

The End

If you enjoyed this story, we'd be grateful if you left an honest online review.

Please turn the page to read the first few chapters of *Deadly Declarations* and *The Plus One*.

DEADLY DECLARATIONS
BY LANDIS WADE

CHAPTER 1
CONCEALMENT

June 22, 1819,

John Adams's Letter to Thomas Jefferson

Dear Sir:

May I enclose to you one of the greatest curiosities and one of the deepest mysteries that ever occurred to me? It is in the Essex Register of June 5, 1819. It is entitled the Mecklenburg Declaration of Independence.

How is it possible that this paper should have been concealed from me to this day?

Had it been communicated to me in the time of it, I know, if you do not know, that it would have been printed in every Whig newspaper upon the continent. You know, that if I had possessed it, I would have made the hall of Congress echo and reecho with it fifteen months before your Declaration of Independence. What a poor, malicious, short-sighted, crapulous mass is Tom Paine's Common Sense, in comparison with this paper.

I am and always shall be affectionately and respectfully yours,
J. Adams

CHAPTER 2
WAKING UP DEAD

Yeager Alexander's motto for retirement living was, "Ain't dead, yet," but when he heard a siren and saw an ambulance, lights flashing, heading for one of the residential buildings at the Independence Retirement Community, he said aloud, "Waking up dead is rarely a good thing." The red and white swirling lights came into view as he finished his pre-dawn walk. This was not the first time he'd seen this vehicle at the Indie. He was sure it wouldn't be the last.

Yeager stood on the crushed gravel path that fronted his cottage and bordered Lost Cove Lake, the smaller of the two Indie lakes. He liked to get up early and walk the land. Around the community center. Past the five-story residence buildings. Between the cottages that fronted Freedom Lake. And across the property line to admire the Hezekiah Alexander Rock House, the jewel of the Queen City History Museum. The house was built in 1774 and had stone siding with strange carvings (if you knew where to look, and Yeager did). It had been home to one of the signers of Mecklenburg County's controversial and long-vanished declaration of independence from Britain, signed on May 20, 1775.

Yeager's best friend, Matthew Collins, was taking him on a road trip in a few hours that had something to do with the Mecklenburg Declaration of Independence. The ninety-six-year-old Collins was known to everyone as the professor because of his love of history. The professor did not believe the Meck Dec had ever existed, but he'd promised Yeager a surprise on their outing, one he said Yeager would like.

What Yeager didn't like was the ambulance being parked in front of the professor's building. He walked the fifty yards up the hill and stopped in the shadows, not twenty feet away from a woman dressed in a medic uniform who was talking on a radio. The early morning air was cool and smelled of pine and rain. Clouds gathered. The quiet before the coming storm allowed the seriousness in her voice to carry on the freshening breeze.

"He's dead. Collecting the body now."

Yeager followed the paramedic into the building and onto the elevator for a ride to the third floor. He let her step out first, held the door until she was out of sight, and slid into the elevator lobby. He peeked around the corner of the narrow hallway and saw her enter room 312, the residence of his best friend. Yeager felt unsteady, like the floor had pitched. He squeezed his eyes shut and reached out to the wall for balance. He bit his lip to suppress the tears he felt coming, but it didn't do much good. He thought of Lori, the professor's granddaughter. She would be heartbroken too.

Minutes later, the paramedic and her partner came out the door of 312, rolling a stretcher that held a covered body.

A woman in a pink silk nightgown and robe walked beside the stretcher. She had her right hand resting on the body's chest. Yeager knew who the woman was, and it was a shock to see her there. He leaned back against the faded green wall. He had nowhere to hide.

The woman's eyes widened when she saw him. "What are you doing here?"

"I saw the ambulance."

Sue Ellen Parker turned away and watched the paramedics load the professor on the elevator.

"Anything I can do?" Yeager said.

She stepped past Yeager onto the elevator and turned around. "People will talk. You should keep your mouth shut." And then for emphasis, as the doors closed, she said, "For once."

Yeager was alone in the quiet of the dim hallway. He wiped his eyes and ran the fingers on his right hand through his thick, tangled beard like a comb. What would people talk about, and what did she want him to keep quiet about?

The professor hadn't mentioned any spend-the-night parties with Sue Ellen, and Yeager hadn't heard any rumors about them. But rumors grew faster than weeds at the Indie and were harder to kill. Still, Yeager didn't believe cohabitation was the issue. He owed it to the professor to find out what secret Sue Ellen really wanted to keep. Yeager took out his key, the one the professor had given him, and let himself in the professor's place.

Yeager wasn't sure what he was looking for, but since the motivation for his unauthorized inspection was the sight of Sue Ellen Parker coming from the professor's unit in the early morning and in her night clothes at that, he started in the master bedroom. The double bed was not the answer. Covers and sheets were pulled back on one side only. The bedside table held a clock, a lamp, and a pill bottle turned on its side, with the cap on the floor and pills spilled on the table and the floor. Yeager inspected the bottle. It was the professor's prescription medication for insomnia.

Yeager opened the closet and found it full of men's slacks, shirts, and sport coats. No woman's clothes in sight. The bathroom was next. Just one toothbrush and cup next to the sink. No blow dryer. Nothing under the sink but a man's Dopp kit and extra shaving lotion.

After his brief search, Yeager surmised the professor bedded down without Sue Ellen Parker at his side. It didn't mean she'd never slept with him. Anything was possible when it came to old-people sex at the Indie, but other than a few pillows and a blanket strewn on the sofa in the great room—the only clue she or somebody else might have spent the night there—Yeager found no other evidence to explain her presence.

Raindrops streaked the large window in the great room. Normally, Yeager liked early morning rain, but this was no mist. Droplets pelted against the pane as limbs on trees swayed. He saw lightning streak and heard thunder boom. It sounded like God was angry. As she should be.

Yeager reached over to the side table and picked up *Trout* magazine. The professor had dog-eared the page with the latest in rod and reel technology. The pictures reminded Yeager of the conversation he'd had with the professor by Freedom Lake three weeks ago, the last time they fished together.

"My fly rod," the professor said, "may not be as efficient as your .22, but it gives the fish a fighting chance." Yeager smiled at the memory.

The professor was a man who never threw away books, even when they were torn and worn. Where there wasn't enough space on the professor's shelves, books spilled onto the floor or were stacked in corners. The one concession he'd made to what seemed at first glance like disorder was how he grouped his books by topic.

The section Yeager liked the best held the Revolutionary War books. Out of habit, he glanced toward his favorite section and was surprised to see empty shelves. Those books were missing, even the books about the Mecklenburg Declaration of Independence.

Yeager was one of the few people who could ask the professor questions about the Meck Dec without the professor getting riled up. Yeager's mother told him there were no stupid questions, so he kept asking them, stupid question after stupid question after stupid question. It made the professor laugh. "Chuck Yeager Alexander, you think you're related to Hezeki-ah," the professor would say. "You want the story to be true."

The professor was right. Yeager did want to believe that local patriots had declared independence from Britain over one year before they got around to it in Philadelphia. He loved the idea, thanks to his mother who had been a high school social studies teacher. Yeager was an only child, because, she'd said, "After you, I didn't have the energy to raise another devil." She was the reason he fell in love with history and the reason he came to the Indie when he was fifty-five years old, to look after her. When she died of cancer, he stayed on and became the youngest resident, despite the hiccup with the business office when they checked his credit. Once they confirmed his mother left him the cottage, the rest of her teacher's pension, and a nice life insurance pay-out, they reluctantly accepted the likes of a man who never would have lived at the Indie were it not for his mother. That was twenty years ago, the same time he struck up his friendship with the professor and the same time he learned about the Meck Dec.

The professor had been adamant the Meck Dec never existed. "It's a fairy tale, nothing more."

But a week ago, in a strange twist, things changed. "Yeager, you can't tell anyone what I am about to tell you. I'm working on a sequel to *An American Hoax.*"

An American Hoax was the professor's bestselling book that debunked the Meck Dec story once and for all. Why did the professor need to write a sequel? What more could he say? It seemed like overkill to say it twice. But Yeager had kept his thoughts to himself when the professor told him about the sequel. Something was different and serious about the professor's behavior that day.

Over the next five days, the professor ordered his meals sent to his room. Every time Yeager checked on him, he was hard at work on his laptop. He said he needed to finish the book before it was too late. He didn't explain the urgency.

Yesterday, Yeager stopped by at lunchtime and the professor was wearing the same clothes from the day before. He hadn't slept, and he'd acted nervous, like he'd had too much coffee. Yeager encouraged him to take a break.

"I can't."

"Why not?"

The professor's nervous energy must have provided a spark. His face lit up. "I found something. Something that changes everything."

Yeager wondered what that meant. Would the professor's sequel reveal the Meck Dec was not a hoax after all? And if so, what had the professor found?

He asked the professor to explain, but the only answer he got was, "Wait until tomorrow. Meet me at eight in the morning. Pack an overnight bag."

Now the professor was dead.

Yeager swept the great room, looking for the professor's laptop. Like the Revolutionary War books, it was nowhere to be found. He approached the open rolltop desk, touched the papers on the desk, and pushed them around. The pile was mostly bills, medical records, and letters from insurance companies. The laptop was not under them.

As he nosed in the pile, he accidentally knocked a piece of paper to the floor. When he picked it up, he saw four words at the top: "Last Will and Testament." It was dated the previous day, within twenty-four hours of the professor's death.

Why did the professor have a will that fit on one sheet of paper? He could afford the most expensive law firm in the city to give away his assets.

Curiosity trumped respect for his friend's privacy as Yeager examined the document under the small lamp on the professor's desk. All the words appeared to be written in the professor's hand. They said:

"I, Matthew Collins, being of sound mind and body, do hereby revoke all prior wills, disinherit my only heir, my grandchild Lori Collins, and bequeath my entire estate to Sue Ellen Parker."

Yeager would have laughed aloud if someone had told him this story in a bar. But here he was, staring nonsense in the face.

The professor said nothing to Yeager about making a new will or anything that would cause him to change the old one. Yeager knew how much the professor loved Lori, and as best Yeager could tell, the professor never loved Sue Ellen Parker. Why would he cut Lori from his will and give his fifty-million-dollar fortune to Sue Ellen? The missing books and laptop bothered Yeager too. They were important to the professor.

Yeager found it hard to accept the professor had fallen in with the likes of Sue Ellen Parker. He was a courageous man who made a pile of money in the magazine business and—a veteran himself—used it to start a foundation for veterans. That was long before finding his passion—or his obsession—as the amateur historian turned famous author who liked to keep to himself.

Sue Ellen Parker was the opposite of reclusive. She was the self-appointed captain of the Indie ship and queen of the biting quip, a snob without an empathetic bone in her body. And while the professor was opinionated about things that truly mattered—like getting history right—she was opinionated about things that didn't matter—like the flower arrangements in the lobby, the color for the carpet renovation, and the uniform style worn by the staff. She gave no quarter to residents who dared disagree with her decorating, renovation, and style judgments and was not a pleasant person to be around, period.

Yeager faced too many questions to tackle them alone. There Sue Ellen was in her pink silk robe, warning him to stay out of—what? The reason she was with the professor when he died? The reason the professor gave her his entire fortune? The reason the professor's history books, laptop, and manuscript on the Meck Deck sequel were missing?

Yeager needed to speak with Harriet Keaton, the smartest and most practical woman he knew. Next to the professor, she was the only resident who treated Yeager like he mattered. She was also the only resident who could take on Sue Ellen Parker.

But Harriet Keaton wasn't a lawyer. They would need a lawyer to know if the will was valid. That gave him an idea.

Yeager's sources among the Indie staff told him the vacant cottage next to him was about to be occupied by a lawyer named Craig Travail. Yeager decided he'd make a good first impression on the man and then secure his help.

CHAPTER 3
TAKE THIS JOB

Craig Travail ripped the envelope open, then gripped the court's ruling in one hand while he used the other to flick a soiled tobacco leaf from the page. It was from the superior court judge's office, and it smelled like chewing tobacco. Chief Judge Roscoe "Chaw" Brady must have sealed it himself. The county had a no smoking policy in public buildings, but Judge Brady found a loophole that led to his nickname and the installation of the gold-plated spittoon under his courtroom bench. Lawyers could measure their impact based on the spittoon's use. The judge spit when he didn't care for your argument, and Judge Chaw Brady spit often during Travail's argument in this case, the biggest case Travail had argued in ten years.

Travail scanned the document, dropped it on his desk, and took a deep breath. He'd lost again. And this time, the dollar amount the firm's client had to pay was staggering.

Rain beat against the ceiling-high window of Travail's skyscraper office like someone tap dancing on his head, and the fog blocked his city view and his next step. It was as if he was short on fuel and flying on instruments when his office phone rang. The extension number on the phone's digital screen belonged to an unfriendly navigator.

"We need to talk." The phone slammed on the other end. The law firm's principal had called Travail to his office.

Travail had an acute feeling his career waging conflict was about to find a resolution at age sixty-five. The management committee of the Am Law 100 law firm, where he'd worked for forty years and been a partner for thirty-three, demanded victories and profits and saw nothing of value in a well-fought contest that came up short, not even when the lawyer did it while dealing with the emotional burden of a family tragedy.

It wasn't so much the law's demands that brought him to this point; it was the natural order of things, where priorities, desires, and competence got sorted out with age.

Why did he continue to practice law? And what was the purpose? These were questions he'd asked himself often during the last two years. And yet he'd kept at it, every day, like a dutiful paper boy, up and at it every morning and never missing his route. He just kept showing up, tackling old and new cases, and filling out his time sheets, because he didn't know what else to do with his life.

It was a problem for trial lawyers his age, and he knew it. They didn't know when to let go, when to let something other than the legal profession define them. They achieved Super Lawyer and Best Lawyer status and thought it gave them special powers. It didn't. It only blinded them to the reality they should do something else with their lives. A lawyer-turned-artist friend explained it best over a pitcher of beer. "Lawyers need to transition to their Act 3 before they turn sixty-five. After that, it's like practicing law at the Hotel California. They can check out, but they can never leave."

No matter how well Travail tried to compartmentalize his personal loss from his work life and how effectively he'd used his courtroom skills, he'd come up short in his last three cases, come in second to be exact, and second was no good for a trial lawyer where first and second places are the only two options. Travail's brain told him he was not a bad trial lawyer, that facts were facts and even the best lawyers lose cases. Yet he knew a losing streak was like a trial lawyer's poison. Clients didn't want to bet on you. And in his case, the firm's managing partner would not allow one more loss.

Did Travail care? Yes, and no. He cared about doing a good job for his clients. He didn't care one lick about pleasing Robert Elkin, the firm's managing partner, who was known by all who worked for him as the biggest jerk of all the jerks who'd held the position.

Travail measured his breath, something he'd learned to do to manage his stress and anxiety. Sometimes the tactic worked, but today, the in-and-out breathing exercise was an irritant, a reminder he was still alive and someone he loved wasn't. He stepped from his office and walked with a regular stride down the east corridor, where the law firm's commercial litigators breathed but barely lived. No one appeared in the hallway to give him encouragement. Solid wood doors with brass handles were shut, with lawyers huddled behind them, typing, dictating, or talking on their phones. Unsociable is what the billable hour had made the uptown lawyer. Not like the old days.

Travail walked past the elevator and into the stairwell,

where he climbed four flights to the forty-fifth floor of the America Bank office tower. When he emerged, he was within view of Elkin's corner office, the one the firm leader used when he worked in Charlotte. He could hear the man yelling through the door. He counted to ten before he knocked and entered.

Charlotte was a New South city where staid law firm traditions had given way to more casual operations. It was why the Charlotte lawyers in the firm called Elkin—behind his back, that is—by a nickname that drew inspiration from Walt Disney's Cruella de Vil. Three clever associates who preferred to remain anonymous coined the nickname based on Elkin's attitude that tradition was important, and Virginia had more of it than North Carolina. He issued most law firm edicts from the Charlottesville office, the city of his birth and education. When he tried to turn the more casual Charlotte into Charlottesville, coat and tie only, solemnly Southern, and everything else old Virginy, he became Robert de Vil.

Elkin and the other two management committee members were waiting for Travail. One, a thin rail of a man named Birdsong who rarely spoke to Travail, reached behind him and closed the door. The other man was Dunkler. He was a bit on the heavy side and always had a dour look on his face.

"Have a seat." Elkin's words came out as a demand.

"I'll stand, thanks."

Elkin came around from behind his expansive mahogany desk with the inlaid gold border and walked to within a Dictaphone's length of Travail's nose, close enough for Travail to smell his breath. He expelled breath that had a caramel flavor with a briny, salt-water touch, the aroma of a pungent cigar with a liquid chaser, most likely, whiskey with an *e*, as Elkin liked to remind the less informed. Elkin's choice of Jefferson's Ocean Aged at Sea Straight Bourbon Whiskey was more about the name on the side of the bottle than it was about drinking whiskey aged in a ship's bow after it traveled the seven seas.

It was ironic, Travail thought, that Thomas Jefferson—who Elkin idolized—didn't like distilled spirits and Elkin lapped them up. Elkin breathed his next question on Travail's face.

"What the hell is this?" Elkin tapped him twice on the shoulder with the rolled paper.

"You know what it is."

"Damn it, Craig, what the hell is wrong with you? Another loss, and for our firm's biggest client."

Travail knew how he wanted to respond. He wanted to say this was no surprise, that "I warned you and I advised the client to settle, but you stepped in and convinced the client it could win." He also wanted to say Elkin's approach was typical of corporate lawyers who knew nothing about litigation, making unrealistic promises and leaving the heavy lifting to the trial lawyers. But Travail kept quiet and let Elkin vent. The man had built up a lot of steam.

While Elkin babbled, Travail glanced at Thomas Jefferson's bust on the pedestal in Elkin's shadow and thought of the speeches Elkin made to the law firm every quarter when he invoked the words and deeds of the former president. He did it to inspire the partners to generate more bucks for the bang. Thomas Jefferson doubled the country's size with a pen's stroke, Elkin would say time and again, "and we can double the firm's size too, if only you think strategically and work hard, as did Jefferson."

Amidst Elkin's droning voice, Travail wondered if Elkin

really was related to the former president, as he liked to claim. Travail doubted it, but he never figured it was worth the trouble to call him on it, nor was it time to pick that fight now.

Birdsong and Dunkler stood still like well-behaved mannequins in a department store window. They added nothing of value to the conversation. Elkin fired at Travail again. "What? No excuses?"

Travail remained silent, which triggered another outburst from Elkin. "You should have retired after the accident."

When Elkin spoke, there was no appendage of "God rest her soul" nor any sympathetic words for Rachael, the wife Travail had grieved for the past two years. They'd married the month before he took the job, and he never thought her life would end before he stopped practicing law. Law was a career, one Travail thought he loved, but that turned out not to be true. Rachael had been his true love and law his true regret. Regret for spending too much time at the office and not enough time with her.

Elkin's insensitivity shook Travail. He'd prepared himself to stand silently while the man blew through his anger. But because of his caustic and uncaring mention of Rachael, as if she were to blame for the case Elkin torpedoed, he felt anger boil deep inside his gut. Until now, it was an emotion he had controlled in Robert Elkin's presence.

Elkin scowled at Travail. "Do you know what kind of hit it will be to our bottom line if we lose this client?"

The bottom line was Robert Elkin's clarion call of progress. To Elkin, law practice was more about collections and billings and prospecting and sales than it was about the flare and excitement of pretending to be the fictional English barrister,

Rumpole of the Bailey. That symbol of change—from noble profession to stark business enterprise—now stood less than one foot away making noise with his mouth and disrespecting Travail's loss of Rachael.

Elkin was four inches taller and bellowed from a frame that had Travail by a good thirty pounds, but Travail was not intimidated. In his younger days, he'd been an undersized but scrappy outside linebacker on his high school football team. That fifty-year-old memory about how to make a solid tackle came into focus as Travail eyed Elkin's silk tie, his frame's center.

The slow building heat in his stomach reached the boiling point. He was not a violent man, but he was human. He needed to stand up for his wife, if he did nothing else right today.

Travail bent his knees, dropped his arms to his sides, and sprang forward like he'd done under the Friday night lights on the gridiron.

"What the—?" Elkin couldn't finish before Travail planted his head in Elkin's chest, wrapped his arms around the managing partner's buttocks, lifted him two feet off the ground, and drove him over the most expensive desk in the law firm. Papers and pens flew in all directions. They toppled the pedestal that held the former commander-in-chief's bust. Thomas Jefferson fell headfirst, glancing off Travail's shoulder and headbutting Elkin. They landed in a stack of Bar Quarterlies.

Birdsong and Dunkler shrieked and dove onto the pile to rescue Elkin. They grabbed Travail by the collar and pulled at him while Elkin, eyes wild with fury, pounced on the former president's head like it was a fumbled pigskin in a Virginia football game. Elkin shouted curses, grabbed at the desk, and pulled himself up with Jefferson's bust cradled in his left arm.

Travail was stunned by the aftermath of his adrenaline surge, but he had perfect vision. De Vil's designer shirt was torn, his hair disheveled, and blood trickled down his brow to the top of his nose.

"You're fired."

"No need. I quit." Travail spoke in a calm voice as he dusted himself off.

"Even better. When you quit, you forfeit your year-end profit share. Your pay ends today."

That was fine. It was a small price to pay to be away from Elkin and those like him. Travail turned his back on the three-some and walked out the door. Elkin yelled at him.

"Insurance ends today too. From now on, you pay for your own therapy. Lot of good it did you."

Travail returned to his office, where he wasted no time packing a few personal files and family pictures in a paperboard box. He slipped his personal laptop in the leather satchel Rachael gave him for his sixtieth birthday. That was the night she pitched the idea of the trip she wanted them to take to visit national parks in an RV. She wanted to go that summer, but he negotiated to wait until he was sixty-three, figuring he'd be closer to retirement and better able to take two months off. Her accident happened two days before they were scheduled to leave. He cancelled the trip, buried Rachael, and went back to work, because he didn't know what else to do.

Travail shook his head as he looked around the work prison he'd built for himself the last two years. He picked up his stuff and walked to the cubicle closest to his office, where he found

Angela, his longtime assistant, sadness etched on her face. News traveled fast through the firm's grapevine.

Travail stumbled through an apology, which she said wasn't necessary. He apologized anyway for leaving her at a job with Elkin in charge. With misty eyes, she smiled a dutiful smile as she dusted some of the grime from Elkin's floor off his shoulders.

"What can I do to help?"

"Please send everything else that belongs to me to the house."

"The new address?"

The reminder made him stop and consider how he had compounded one transition—the end of his law career—with another, his move from the place he and Rachael had called home. Only Angela, his two grown children, and his therapist knew he'd bought a small cottage at the Independence Retirement Community.

"I'm not retiring," he'd told Angela. "I just need less space." The statement was half true. He needed less space, but his therapist and adult children had urged him to move out of the shadow of loss and into the light.

"Yes." He shrugged. "Send everything to the new address."

"Did you hear Professor Collins died this morning? It was on the radio."

He hadn't heard. It was not a shock though. Professor Collins had to be in his mid-nineties. But the news made him think about his prior representation of the professor, and he could hear the professor's voice in his head like it was yesterday. "Of course I did my own work."

Fifteen years earlier, he'd handled a defamation case for the professor. A newspaper ran a story saying the professor committed plagiarism in *An American Hoax*. Travail had taken the case at the urging of Elkin, who for some reason, loved the professor's book. The jury came back with a ten-million-dollar verdict for the professor.

"Strange coincidence, the professor died the same day you move to the Indie," Angela said.

Not so strange. One dies. Another takes his place. Circle of life. But it caused Travail to reflect. The professor had been indignant when he'd shown Travail around his Indie condo. "Do you think this is the library of a man lazy enough to copy work from other people?"

The shelves in the professor's great room were more cluttered than Travail's garage, but with papers and books, not lawn and sports equipment. The mess helped Travail prove to the jury the professor had done the hard work of researching and writing the book himself, a man obsessed with his topic.

"You don't think his death had anything to do with the Meck Dec, do you?" Angela had always enjoyed a good mystery. It was why she was such an excellent assistant, always asking "what if" when Travail was stumped on a case. Her eyes sparkled when she asked the question and her grin was wide, as if she were trying to create a distraction to take his mind off his last day at the law firm.

Professor Collins had made enemies at the chamber of commerce and the May 20th Society by denying the Meck Dec was real, but the friction's source was couched in local tourism and historical debate, hardly enough to warrant foul play. His detractors didn't like the fervor of his ultimate conclusion in *An American Hoax*, which the professor insisted was fact, not opinion. He also became the go-to guy every May 20 for a soundbite for media outlets in any cities jealous of Charlotte's growth and economic success. "Is there any truth to the story," they would ask, "that the first declaration of independence from Great Britain was signed in Charlotte on May 20, 1775?" The professor, clutching his *New York Times* bestselling book, would put on a show, saying "absolutely not" every time, with a great deal of passion and enthusiasm.

"I'm sure it was old age," Travail said. "He was ninety-something. As for the Meck Dec, it is just an interesting bit of disputed local history, and as far as I'm concerned, rather insignificant history in the twenty-first century."

"Still, I have to wonder." Angela opened the satchel on his shoulder and stuffed "something you might need" inside.

Travail hugged her tight. "Thanks for everything you've done for me."

Five minutes later, he departed the elevator into the parking deck and walked away from the law firm where he'd devoted his entire legal career. He was now convinced there was no higher purpose to helping big companies win legal battles. And yet, he felt a touch of sadness. Law practice was all he knew how to do to make a living. It was all he knew how to do, period. It was his identity. Who was he now?

The motor in his aging sedan came to life as he had a feeling he was about to be buried alive among people with nothing to do. He was convinced they would turn him into a do-nothing clone. And it was only 11:00 am.

When he left the parking lot, the storm had passed, but the pavement was wet. He glanced at the sunlit Carolina blue sky, but it didn't feel sunny or bright. He lowered both front windows and touched the radio to try to turn off the noise. Instead, he accidentally changed the channel. A disc jockey on a country music station thanked God it was Friday and introduced an old favorite by Johnny Paycheck, "Take This Job and Shove It." As the song's refrain filled the air, he couldn't help himself. He let slip a half-hearted smile and hummed along. The country music gods had a sense of humor.

A fresh breeze blew through the front windows as Travail turned left onto Third Street, crossed Tryon, and sped through one green city stoplight after another. He nodded at the courthouse, passed under the I-277 loop, and cut over to Independence Boulevard, his pathway to the Indie. On the way, he would pick up his four-legged best friend from the old house and let Blue ride shotgun to the new one.

At the song's finale, Travail spoke a question to the radio. "Was it worth it, Johnny?"

The musician didn't answer. It was no matter. Travail figured it wouldn't be long before the Indie answered the question for him.

To read more, you can order *Deadly Declarations* in print, eBook, or audiobook, wherever books are sold.

Learn more at <u>landiswade.com.</u>

THE PLUS ONE

BY SARAH ARCHER

<h1 style="text-align:center">CHAPTER ONE</h1>

Of the three people standing onstage, only two of them were people. But that was totally normal to Kelly—one of the *people* people. Along with Priya, her best friend and fellow robotics engineer (the other *person* person), she looked out over the audience filling the brightly lit demonstration room: a field trip of fifty or so kids, squirming and grouchy under the cloud of that early January gloom. The children were freshly reinstitutionalized after two halcyon weeks of holiday break, the feral spirit of pajama days and pumpkin pie breakfasts still smoldering in their eyes. And now it was up to Kelly to win their wandering attention.

"I'd like you to meet Zed," she began tentatively, gesturing to the robot standing beside her. He was one of the first projects she had worked on five years ago when she had landed her coveted job at Automated Human Industries, AHI, *the* boutique cutting-edge robotics company. Zed made a modest impression at first glance, his body a four-foot-tall construction of steel ligaments and exposed wires, his face a flat panel. "I know he looks pretty basic," she continued, trying and failing to eclipse the gleeful Pillsbury Doughboy noises issuing from four girls in the back as they took turns poking each other's stomachs. Kelly was not the most confident performer. This was a young woman who, when playing a tree in her third-grade play, had gotten stage fright—despite not having any lines—and dramatically fled the theater. Which had not been easy, seeing as her legs had been bound together in a trunk.

But now her voice grew as she got excited, talking about her work. "But at the point of his creation, Zed had a greater scope of motion capabilities than anything else on the market. He was our first build with our patented predictive stereo vision—"

A tinny ring from the front row announced that a sandy-haired boy had just won a game on his contraband phone—and threw Kelly off her flow. Robbie, one of her coworkers here at AHI, bustled over and extended a hand. "Phone," he commanded. The boy dutifully dropped his thousand-dollar smartphone into a red plastic bucket of other thousand-dollar smartphones, glass hitting metal with a thump. Robbie had jumped at the chance to play phone wrangler today, ensuring that—even though none of the company's newest technology was on display—no junior spies filmed the program for their parents, two thirds of whom probably worked at competing tech companies here in Silicon Valley. He clutched the bucket with a sort of protective satisfaction and retreated to his position at the sidelines, from which he watched the rows of children like a prison guard. Sometimes Kelly couldn't believe that she had dated him.

She refocused. She was determined to get through to these students. Or at least to half of them. Maybe one? Just a small one? But so many were talking to each other that they could barely hear her. The whole detailed presentation she had perfected and rehearsed was falling apart in practice. "So we started with something called stochastic mapping, which is, um —" She faltered. Her eyes darted irresistibly toward the exit. She felt another "fleeing tree" moment coming on.

"It's kind of easier if you see it first," Priya gently interrupted. "Who wants to see this guy in action?"

"Yeah!" a couple of the kids responded, sitting up. Kelly relaxed as she looked across at her friend, grateful for the intervention. Priya was better at this type of thing anyway. She could get a smile out of a statue.

"Shall you do the honors, madam?" she asked now.

"I shall, mademoiselle." Kelly clicked the remote in her hand and Zed beeped into life, his blue eyes blinking on. More of the children looked up, their attention caught. "So he can walk, of course." She pushed the mini joystick on the remote forward and Zed took a few steps, his movements more fluid than his rough form seemed to indicate.

"But big deal, right?" Priya asked the crowd. "You guys have been walking for years." Some of the kids giggled.

"But he can also walk *sideways*, which is pretty cool." Kelly toggled to the right on the remote, sending Zed into a side-to-side grapevine movement. "And if you add in the arms—"

Priya pressed a sequence of buttons on her own remote and the robot added a rhythmic arm movement to his routine. "Zed's got some major moves." The kids in the audience started clapping.

"Observe." Kelly swept the joystick around, and Zed whirled in a perfect, whip-fast pirouette, stopping on a dime. The sandy-haired boy let out an involuntary "Whoa!"

"Way better than my moves, I have to admit," Kelly said.

As the crowd laughed and cheered, Kelly sneaked a grin at Priya. They had officially won these kids over with the sweet smell of science. They were superheroes. Now she spoke confidently as she started to explain her process. This was her favorite part: the magic of engineering, the ability to imagine an impossible-to-solve problem, then slowly break it down, unpiecing it until it became possible.

"So how do you teach a robot to walk?" she asked the crowd. They were silent now, utterly rapt. "Imagine you were trying to give someone else the ability to walk for the first time. What would you need to give him?"

"Feet!" one child cried.

"Good, that's the first thing." She was actually starting to enjoy this. "What would those feet need to be able to do?"

But the buzz of another phone, conspicuous in the quiet, cut her off. Her eyes shot instinctively to Robbie, waiting for him to nab the culprit. But Robbie's glare was fixed squarely on her. "I'm so sorry," she muttered, fumbling her own phone out of her pocket and striking the Ignore button. She could almost physically feel everyone watching.

It had been her mom calling, but she could have guessed that even without looking at the screen. It was *always* her mom calling. She cleared her throat and tried to resume the presentation, but she had lost her train of thought. "So . . . the feet. The feet would need to be able to balance flat on the ground, right? What else?"

She felt a smaller rumble in her pocket as a voicemail registered, where it would sit alongside the five or six other voicemails from her mother that could be found on Kelly's phone at all times. She could already hear what this one would say: "Are you coming to family dinner this weekend?" (Yes, Kelly came to every family dinner, every two weeks like clockwork.) And "Are you bringing a date?" (No, it's a family dinner, that would be weird.) Of course, Kelly was rarely dating anyone anyway. But that wasn't the point.

Diane's energetic voice filled Kelly's mind so loudly that she failed to hear the kids shouting answers at her in the audience. "Sorry, what? One at a time," she said. Just moments ago she had been doing so well. She had asked her mom time and time again to not call while she was at work, but Diane just never seemed to think that Kelly's work was too important to interrupt. "How about balance?" she tried again. "Wait, I just said that. Um—"

Priya gave her a sympathetic glance before stepping forward again. "What did you just say? You, the boy in the awesome Spiderman shirt? That the feet have to talk to the brain? That's right. You have to figure out how those feet are going to know what to do."

This time Kelly stepped back, allowing Priya to take over for her. She had lost the nerve to try again.

The drive from AHI to her parents' house that Sunday wasn't far. But passing from the sweeping, glass-bound corporate giants of North San Jose to the leafy suburban streets of Willow Glen always gave her the feeling of entering another world. Maybe she became more of the girl she was growing up there, less of the woman she was now.

The Suttle house was a neat ranch-style home that looked as modestly middle class as ever despite the million-dollar price tag the tech boom had hung on it. The sage-green painted exterior was nice enough, framed by solid bushes and a white bench tucked beneath a shady oak tree, but it gave way to an interior that had, in the decades-long war of attrition that was her parents' marriage, become almost entirely her mother's territory. Pillows with an indefensible number of tassels, framed flower prints jockeying for wall space, a menagerie of china and glass figurines—Diane had difficulty saying no to anything beautiful, or at least cute, or at least, well, whatever was appealing about the life-sized sculpture of a cat that glowered at them from the mantel. Family portraits from years gone by had the five Suttles smiling down, pressed and perfect, from every room. But the actual family tableaus formed in these rooms were never so idyllic. Kelly took a heavy breath as she entered the house. Something about the numerous clashing pots of potpourri, the unidentifiable cooking smells, the thick fug of repressed childhood emotions, made the air more difficult to breathe here. Kelly loved her family. But sometimes she thought it would be easier to love them if she didn't have a career that kept her so close.

As she emerged into the kitchen, she looked to see what her mother was cooking, but her spirits fell when she saw her ladling an ominous, gelatinous something onto plates. The older she got, the more Diane embraced a sort of culinary Russian roulette, throwing ingredients together with abandon, and the results were as likely to be toxic as inspired. Kelly could already tell that tonight would be a miss. Meanwhile, Diane talked a stream to Clara, Kelly's twenty-five-year-old sister.

Clara had a Disney princess thing going on: she wasn't a super-model, but with wide, round eyes and a sunny smile, she was the sort of pretty that made babies smile at her automatically in checkout lines and customers at the vintage boutique where she worked want to give her the sale. Her strawberry blond head bobbed, listening raptly, while she pushed some parbaked rolls into the oven. Beside her, her fiancé Jonathan, an overgrown but good-natured jock getting soft in the middle since college, dutifully pretended to be doing something with the butter to look busy.

Across the kitchen, Kelly's older brother, Gary, was half visible under his young daughters, who were summiting him like mountain goats. Kelly knew that there were three of them —triplets, in fact—but sometimes suspected he had picked up an extra one somewhere, like a leaf stuck to his hair. They made way too much sound for three humans and with the way they ran around, really, who could tell how many there were, or what was happening at all? It was like that game where you try to guess which cup the penny is under. The only possible solution is that there's a secret fourth cup. They were just reaching the age at which they were developing truly distinct personalities, and Kelly was half thrilled at watching their minds blossom, half terrified at the notion that all three girls could now run and turn doorknobs.

"I talked to the florist about the camellias," Diane was saying as she fluttered around the kitchen, her sleeve of bracelets clinking, her dark hair motionless in its eternally perfect coif. Clara's wedding, which was eight weeks away, was the topic du jour—it was the topic du *every* jour, taking the place of the gossipy stories that Diane usually recounted from Blush, the bridal shop she ran. "It's vital that she understand. Gary, can you grab me the salad tongs?" Diane didn't seem to notice that Gary currently had a shoe in one hand, an upside-down toddler in the other, and an Anna from *Frozen* doll in his mouth. Kelly dove into the room and scooped up the toddler while Gary seamlessly plucked the tongs from their container.

"Ah, Kelly, you're here, finally. Hand me the lettuce spinner?"

Kelly struggled to perch her niece on her hip while extricating the lettuce spinner from a top shelf.

"So if we go with peach, that would mean—"

"White for the ribbons," Diane finished Clara's sentence. "And then—"

"Those other sashes for the bridesmaids, exactly," said Clara.

"The ones you showed me a while ago?" Kelly asked.

"Which were those again?" Clara said, busily setting the butter on the table while Kelly offered the lettuce spinner rather aimlessly, trying to catch her mom's attention. Diane seemed to have forgotten that she wanted it in the first place.

"Um, I don't know, they were in a catalogue?"

"They're all in catalogues, Kelly," Diane asserted. "Don't worry about it, we'll tell you what to wear on the day." Kelly set the lettuce spinner on the counter and pulled her niece closer to her instead, making her laugh with a funny face. She sensed that her energies were better expended there.

"Oh, hi, Dad," she said, just noticing her father. His stillness in the whirl of motion around him had camouflaged him into the room.

"Hi, Kel," he responded, not looking up from his white paper. Carl was always reading or scratching at something for his job as a civil engineer with the local water utility, but he never discussed his work with the family. For someone who worked so closely with technology, he spent an awful lot of time doing things the analogue way, and Kelly suspected this was because of Diane's strict "no devices at dinnertime" policy. If he was working on a notepad, Kelly's mom interpreted it as legitimate and let it slide.

Kelly's father was one of those fifty-five-year-old men with a beard and glasses who looked like he was born a fifty-five-year-old man with a beard and glasses. Trying to imagine him as a young boy, a twenty-year-old, even, was ludicrous. His crescent of close-cut, early whitened hair never seemed to grow, get cut, or fall out. His favorite armchair was so molded to the angles of his body that he didn't sit in it so much as wear it. And in the same way, he wore his marriage to Kelly's mom. When they met, he was studying biochemistry, she theater. They were married before they graduated. A boiling, opposites-attract passion carried them through the first few years. By the time it cooled, Gary was there, and so was a mortgage, and a long future that seemed pretty much planned out. Diane's silliness and flair for the dramatic didn't age well, and Carl's analytical intelligence became boring. They were married now more out of habit than love, though he never appeared to notice such things.

Diane thought often of such things, but was so willfully romantic that she saw only a long and happy marriage, a model for all the young brides-to-be at her shop. So she chattered on blissfully oblivious to her husband's disregard, which was probably the secret to their "success." She focused on the perfect image of her marriage in their family portraits and Carl focused on his work, neither looking at the flesh-and-blood spouse in front of their eyes.

Growing up in such a household, Kelly, an innately rational little girl, had had no choice but to review the evidence of her parents' marriage and conclude that fairy tales were a load of fluff and bunk. With such a mismatched model of love, relationships had always seemed to her at best illogical, at worst a source of pain. And so she poured herself into her Legos, which turned into computers, which turned into intricate robotics systems. Machines made far more sense than people.

While the family ate dinner, or worked the chicken around on their plates to make it look eaten, the topic of conversation was, of course, still Clara's wedding. Several important facts were established. Gary's wife, Gina, an ER nurse with an insane schedule who couldn't be here because she was working, because she was always working, hadn't gotten a dress yet so, yes, Gary had picked out something for her that was color-scheme appropriate. Yes, Jonathan had passed Diane's hair advice (instructions) on to his groomsmen, and it was duly received. And yes, Carl would take a dancing lesson for the father-daughter dance. This was news to Carl.

"A dancing lesson? It's a wedding, not a cabaret."

"Carl, this is your only daughter's wedding—"

Kelly looked around the table to see if anyone else noticed. They didn't.

"And you're going to learn to dance," Diane said in her "I mean business" voice. Carl's face stiffened, even his glasses stiffened, but Clara cut in in a gentler tone, her eyes glimmering with sincerity.

"It's just one lesson, Dad, and it'll make things so much

easier. This way you won't get up there at the wedding and feel like you don't know what to do. You'll have learned everything beforehand; you won't even have to think about it."

"Oh, fine, that's all right then," Carl grumbled. Kelly gulped on her chicken. How did Clara do that? How did she always say the right thing?

But she was quickly distracted by the inevitable question. "So, Kelly," her mom asked brightly, "have you met anyone recently?"

"Well, a boatswain from the Philippines just asked me to connect on LinkedIn, so . . ."

"You know what I mean, a man!"

"No, Mom, since you asked me last week, I have not found a husband."

"No need to be snippy. I just want what's best for you. After all, you are already twenty-nine; I would think you would gladly take my help in the situation. And luckily for you, I met someone!"

"Congratulations, dear. Will I be invited to the wedding?" Carl asked, not looking up from his salad.

"I mean for Kelly, obviously."

"Mom, I don't—"

"Oh, is this the one you were telling me about?" Clara interrupted Kelly excitedly. "I think you'll actually like him, Kel."

"Please don't—" But Kelly failed again.

"Give it a try. Worst that happens is this stranger murders you on the first date, and then at least you're not dying alone," Gary said, slicing food for two of the girls across his own untouched plate. His expression was so straight that few people but Kelly would have been able to tell he was joking. And even she wasn't convinced.

"I really don't want—"

But now Diane cut across Kelly. "Will everyone please just let me finish?" Oh, how rude of me, Kelly thought. "His name is Martin and he's Donna's sister's neighbor's son. He's a realtor and a tennis player and just adorable and best of all, he's the same height as Gary, so everything will be symmetrical in the pictures!"

"What pictures?" Gary asked.

"At the wedding, obviously."

Kelly couldn't let this go on. "Mom, I don't care how good this guy looks next to Gary, I'm not marrying him."

"Not your wedding, silly. Though who knows! I mean for Clara's wedding. Oh, and I almost forgot. He has a cocker spaniel." Diane sat back, satisfied. The man had a cocker spaniel.

"It's perfect, right, Kel?" Clara beamed.

"Wait, so you guys just went and found a plus one for me?"

"I know how you dread these things," Diane said. "Now you don't even have to worry about it."

"What makes you think I don't already have one?"

"Well, you don't—do you?"

Kelly spluttered. "That's not the point! I don't want to go to my sister's wedding with some tennis-playing jerkoff I don't even know."

"But you will know him. I set up dinner for the two of you. You've got almost two months to get to know each other."

Kelly looked to her father. "Dad, you'll pose next to me in

the pictures, right, so everything looks good? I don't need a plus one?"

"I would, but I probably wouldn't live up to your mother's standards. She's never called me adorable."

"Gary? Is anyone going to stand up for me or is my whole family happy to just pimp me out to a strange man off the streets?"

"Honestly, I'd be thrilled to have another guy at the family table," Gary admitted. "My doctor said if I don't start exposing myself to people other than Gina and the girls, I will lactate."

"Kelly, this is ridiculous. You have to bring someone," Diane insisted.

"Why? Who cares?"

"Who cares?" Diane set down her fork. Kelly sensed that she had asked the wrong question. "A wedding is a house of cards, Kelly. If you mess up my seating arrangements, all hell will break loose. And all of my friends, my family, my industry colleagues will be there. The eyes of the Bay Area are on me. I am a bridal professional and this is my daughter's wedding! This is my Triple Crown!"

"Wait, so are you the horse in this scenario?" Kelly couldn't resist asking.

"I think she's the jockey." Gary caught her eye before looking away, masking a grin.

"Please, just give him a chance, Kel," Clara said. "It's one dinner. I think you'll have more fun at the wedding if you have someone to talk to, and I won't have to worry about whether you're having a good time. Please? For me?"

Kelly sighed. Clara's sweet tone was much harder to say no

to than her mother's quasi-mania. She had a feeling she was about to meet a cocker spaniel.

To read more, you can order *The Plus One* in print, eBook, or audiobook, wherever books are sold.

Learn more at saraharcherwrites.com.

ACKNOWLEDGEMENTS

We interviewed several authors on *Charlotte Readers Podcast* who cowrote books together and we thought it would be fun to give cowriting a try. Our thanks to you the reader for taking a chance on our combined effort to make podcasting more mysteriously dangerous.

We're grateful to Kevin Carlock, David Marino, PJ Alexander, Hannah Larrew, and Janet Wade for their feedback on this story, and to Nora Gaskin, Jenifer Ruff, and Bobby Nash for their input on the story and clever blurbs. They helped us make this story better.

Thanks to Tim Barber at Dissect Designs for the cover, Jennipher Tripp for the book design, and Bill A. Jones for narrating the audiobook. They are the fantastic team who pulled the parts and pieces together.

We invite you to learn more about our writing at saraharcherwrites.com and landiswade.com.

We also invite you to listen to *Charlotte Readers Podcast,* where we interview authors and talk about books and writing. You can listen to *Charlotte Readers Podcast* wherever you like to get your podcasts or at charlottereaderspodcast.com. If you'd like to keep up with what we're doing on the podcast, you can sign up for our newsletter at the podcast website.

ABOUT THE AUTHORS

Sarah Archer

Sarah's debut novel, *The Plus One*, was published by Putnam in the US and received a starred review from Booklist. It has also been published in the UK, Germany, and Japan, and is currently in development for television.

As a screenwriter, Sarah has developed material for MTV Entertainment, Snapchat, and Comedy Central. She is a Black List Screenwriting Lab fellow who has placed in competitions including the Motion Picture Academy's Nicholl Fellowship and the Tracking Board's Launch Pad.

Her short stories and poetry have been published in numerous literary magazines, and she has spoken and taught on writing to groups in several states and countries.

Sarah has served as a cohost of *Charlotte Readers Podcast* since June 2022, where she has interviewed authors and shared her knowledge on writing and publishing.

Learn more about Sarah and her writing at saraharcherwrites.com.

Landis Wade

Landis's novel, *Deadly Declarations,* won ten awards, including Winner in the 2022 American Fiction Awards and the National Indie Excellence Awards in the mystery categories.

He is a recovering trial lawyer (after 35 years of law practice) and founder of *Charlotte Readers Podcast* (where he has conducted more than 500 author interviews), whose third book —*The Christmas Redemption*—won the Holiday category of the National Indie Excellence Awards.

His short work has been featured in *Writersdigest.com, The Charlotte Observer, Flying South,* and in several anthologies, and his short story "The Deliberation" won the 2016 North Carolina Bar short story contest. He is a past board member of Charlotte Writers Club.

With the help of Sarah Archer and his other podcast cohost, Hannah Larrew, he published *The Write Quotes* series, an eight-book collection of inspirational and practical quotes by authors from 33 U.S. states and five countries about writing and the writing life.

Learn more about Landis and his writing at landiswade.com.

Learn more about *Charlotte Readers Podcast* at charlottereader spodcast.com.

www.ingramcontent.com/pod-product-compliance
Lightning Source LLC
Chambersburg PA
CBHW020042310726
48970CB00007B/2369